JEEZ AND THE GENTILE

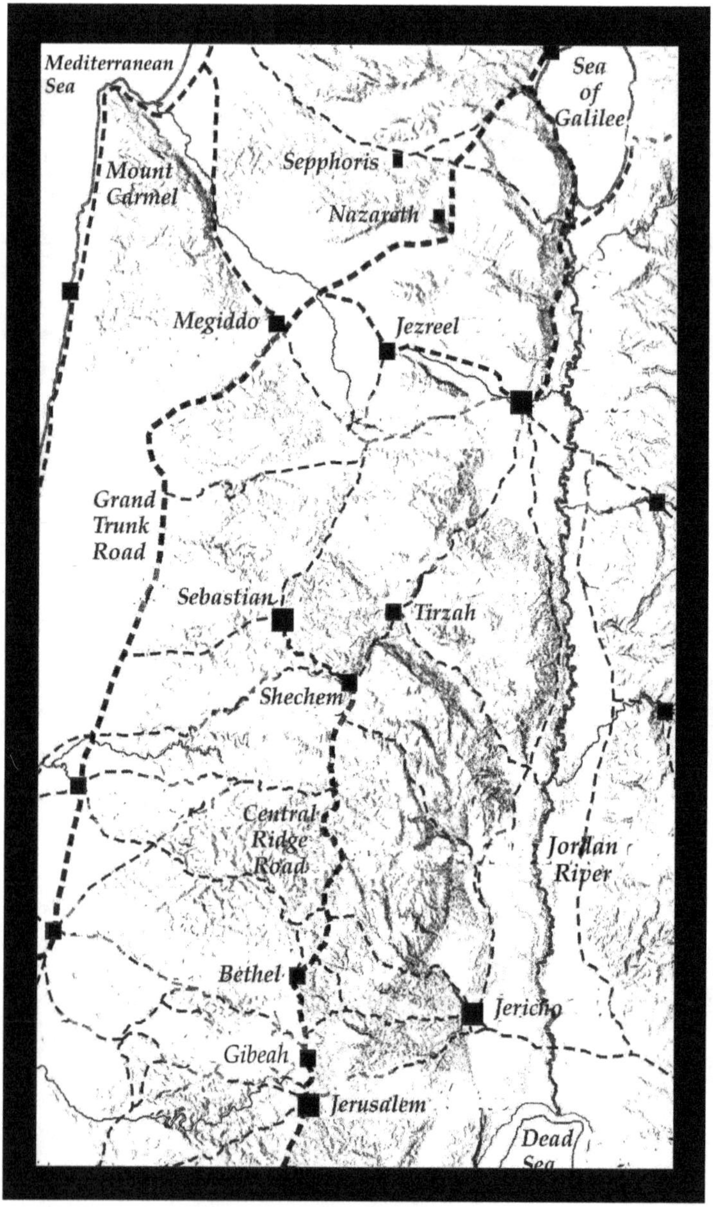

Map of Ancient Israel

JEEZ AND THE GENTILE

Stephen W. Hiemstra

T2P

T2PNEUMA PUBLISHERS LLC
CENTREVILLE, VIRGINIA

Jeez and the Gentile

ISNI: 0000-0000-2902-8171

T2Pneuma Publishers LLC
P.O. Box 230564, Centreville, Virginia 20120
www.T2Pneuma.com

Names: Hiemstra, Stephen W., 1953-, author.
Title: Jeez and the gentile / Stephen W. Hiemstra.
Description: Centreville, VA: T2Pneuma Publishers LLC, 2025.
Identifiers: LCCN: | ISBN: 978-1-942199-51-9 (paperback) | 978-1-942199-67-0 (KDP) | 978-1-942199-93-9 (ePUB)
Subjects: LCSH Jesus Christ--Fiction. | Time travel--Fiction. | Grief--Fiction. | Palestine--Social life and customs--To 70 A.D. | Coming of age--Fiction. | Christian fiction. | BISAC YOUNG ADULT FICTION / Religious / Christian / Action & Adventure | YOUNG ADULT FICTION / Social Themes / Religion & Faith | YOUNG ADULT FICTION / Historical / Middle East
Classification: LCC PS3608 .I46 J44 2025 | DDC 813.6--dc23

Many thanks to my editors Jean Arnold, Sarah Hamaker, Rebecca Norris Resnick, Harim Sanchez, and Nathan Snow.

ACT ONE

Chapter 1

On a Thursday evening in mid-September at his home in McLean, Virginia, a dour twelve-year old Thomas Timmerman played a noisy shoot-em-up game on his laptop in his room when he received a text from perky girl-friend, Maddie.

> Maddie: *How's it going?*
>
> Tom: *The usual. I'm bored.*
>
> Maddie: *Join us for prayer at the flagpole on Wednesday?*
>
> Tom: *How did prayer help my dad? I need a tangible God or I will burst.*
>
> Maddie: *How about a tangible person who believes in God? … I'll be there.*
>
> Tom: *Good for you.*
>
> Maddie: *Later.*

With tears in his eyes, Tom glanced up at the photo on his desk of him and Maddie standing in front of the lion compound at the zoo. The photo recorded the hot day, him in a tie shirt with baseball cap in hand displaying his recent crew cut and her with shoulder length hair over a bright, floral print summer dress.

Feeling sorry for himself, he went on to play on the computer past midnight. Remembering stories his father told when they went shooting together, he thought, *that's not how a police raid would be set up and run*. Slamming his laptop shut, he went to bed.

∞

A Roman centurion contracted Joseph, the carpenter, in mid-September to install a ritual bath in his home in the Galilean city of Sepphoris in AD 9. Standing in front of the household Friday afternoon, Joseph sent his son home to Nazareth for *Shabbat* the week before *Yom Kippur*. A welcome breeze relieved the heat but kicked up dust.

"Take my wages, these seven denarii, and this goat to you mother." Joseph hands the goat's leash to his attentive son, Jeez.

"Yes, father. What do I tell mother about the goat?" Jeez asked.

"Augustine feels guilty for making me work on Shabbat to keep that young Tribune happy." Joseph responded.

"Claudius Lysias, the young Tribune who recently arrived from Rome?" Jeez asked.

Joseph paused to look at Jeez. "The goat is a peace offering for your mother, Mary, who Augustine knows from synagogue" Joseph said.

"Between the bath and respecting *Shabbat*, Augustine is a changed man since he became a god fearer," Jeez commented.

"We should all take God so seriously," Joseph concluded.

Jeez nodded. He walked home to Nazareth before sunset with the goat, a backpack, and a gourd hanging around his neck filled with water.

The evening of the Sabbath and the following evening, the son slept on a woven mat on the roof of their home and rose three hours before dawn. On rising Sunday morning, he drew water from the cistern, washed his face and hands dressed only in a tunic, a long shirt with a belt. Standing under the front-room canopy next to his father's workbench, he broke barley flat bread and ate it with goat-milk cheese dipped in olive oil.

Once he had eaten, his mother, Mary, gave him a

freshly washed cloak, which he put on along with his sandals. He picked up his backpack and shepherd's gourd with water. Finally, as an obedient son, he kissed his mother goodbye and began the trek to Sepphoris.

∞

At seven a.m. Friday morning, Tom's mother knocked on his bedroom door. "Okay, sleepy-head, time to get up. You're late again and will miss the bus."

Tom rolled out of bed and onto the floor still wearing the jeans and a now-sweaty tee shirt from the night before. Tom smelled his tee shirt and made a face.

"Are you okay?" his mother asked.

"I'm up … sort of," Tom replied.

"Get dressed and comb your hair."

"Okay, okay."

"Don't forget your books."

Hair uncombed, Tom picked up his backpack and proceeded down the stairs to the kitchen. He grabbed a bagel on the counter and headed out the front door. Seeing the bus pull up at the end of the cul-de-sac, he threw the backpack over his shoulder and ran to meet it.

∞

After getting razzed for his unkept look by students on the bus, when Tom arrived at school he ducked into the men's room before going to homeroom to freshen up. Looking in the mirror, he began combing his hair when a shifty-looking classmate came up and stood next to him.

"Got any pharmaceutical needs this morning?" the classmate asked.

Tom blew up and began punching him and pushing him up against the wall.

"What's your problem, man?"

Ignoring the question, Tom continued punching him.

Dropping his backpack on the floor, the classmate turned and ran out of the men's room. When the door closed, Tom kicked it into one of the stalls and walked out.

Word got around about the bathroom incident.

Other students gossiped and gave Tom blank stares the rest of the day. Everyone—that is, everyone but the one—understood exactly why Tom blew up, but no one said a thing.

Chapter Two

Saturday morning, Tom's mother let him sleep in until eight. She could not understand how he could sleep with the roar of motorcycles passing in front of their house. He did not stir when she knocked, so she shook him gently to wake him. "Rise and shine."

"It's Saturday."

"You forget. We need to get ready for the funeral. How could you not wake up with the rolling honor guard rehearsing on the parade route? Shower, dress, and come downstairs. I'm making pancakes." She said as she retreated out of the room.

"I'm right on it," Tom turned over and pulled the quilt over his head, unable to face his dad's passing.

His mother waited at the door for a minute, but heard not a sound. "Tom?"

"Okay, okay." Tom rolled out of bed, leaned on the dresser, and stumbled into the bathroom.

"The limo is scheduled to arrive at nine."

∞

At ten o'clock, Tom arrived by limousine with his mother and sister for the viewing at the front of the church sanctuary. Inside, an organist quietly played familiar hymns. In front of the sanctuary, a casket lay open with his father decked out in his police uniform. White floral arrangements and tall, lavender candles were positioned on either side of the casket, adding both a visual aesthetic and an aromatherapy stress abatement.

Tom felt cold and began to shiver, seeing his father lying there with his hat on, eyes closed, and hands wearing white gloves. His mother stood behind him grasping his shoulders, suppressing tears. No one said anything. After spending a few minutes in front of the casket, Tom retreated with his mother and twin sister to sit in the front pew as others filed by. Some stopped and cried. Others walked by slowly and shook his mother's hand. Most proceeded to find a seat, but a few sheepishly wandered to the back, signed the visitor's log, and left.

At eleven o'clock, the pastor began his invocation and offered a prayer. These initiated the familiar rituals of a law enforcement funeral service that included both sacred and secular speakers. Tom knew the drill and anticipated that he would have trouble focusing amid the debilitating sadness and raging anger that blazed through his mind.

In his opening remarks, the pastor reminded the congregation of officer Timmerman's first name. Nicholas is Greek for victory of the people, but the name Timmerman is ethnic Dutch and means: Carpenter. Nicholas died in the line of duty in a raid that captured a record volume of fentanyl, saving countless lives. Unfortunately, the drug dealer who shot him evaded capture.

Tom stiffened up. Crowd stirs audibly.

At this, a bagpiper began playing *Going Home*.

Thus began the lengthy law enforcement funeral liturgy. A police captain said: "Nick led by example. He was known among officers as the policeman's policeman." The county chair recounted: "Nick always showed up for community events and brought other officers with him." A domination official cited John 15:13: "Great love has no one this, that someone lay down his life for his friends." The police chaplain introduced him as: "A son, husband, father, friend, colleague, leader in community." And so it went . . . The bagpiper played again.

When the music stopped, Tom's twin sister stepped forward to the pulpit on the right holding back tears and read the sermon text, "The Lord is my shepherd, I shall not want. . . . Even though I walk through the valley of the shadow of death, I will fear no evil." She takes a breath and swallows. "I will fear no evil, for you are with me; your rod and your staff, they comfort me." (Ps 23:1,4) When she finished, she returned to her seat next to Tom, and the pastor walked up to the pulpit on the left and began his eulogy. Grieved, stressed, and overwhelmed, Tom leaned against his mother and nodded off.

∞

Tom woke in a Sunday morning twilight leaning against a stone pine, one of many, along a walkway up the hill. As he stirred, the flapping of wings alerted him to a turtle dove that came to rest on a branch in the tree above. When he opened his eyes, a young man his age dressed in a robe with sandals stands in front of him.

"Who are you?" Tom asked.

"Most people call me Jeez," The young man responded.

"Clever name. I'm Tom. How did I get here?"

"It looks like you got tired of walking the road to Sepphoris and picked a comfortable tree to take a rest."

"Little chance of that."

"Okay. Call it a divine appointment."

"Divine appointment? What? No blue eyes and long blond hair?"

"Ha, ha. Aren't short, curly, dark hair and brown eyes tangible enough?"

Tom catches himself. "The last thing I remember was the boring funeral service for my father."

"Never mind. Take my hand." Jeez lifted Tom up. "I need your company for a few days."

∞

A pair of hooded crows circle overhead, calling out loudly.

When he finished speaking, four Roman auxiliaries on horseback trotted down the walkway trailing a gagged and bound young woman with long black hair on a donkey. Tom peered into her terrified, green eyes as the rising sun illuminated her face. *Who is this woman? She obviously needs help.*

When the leader saw Jeez, he halted his pale horse and drew his sword with a blooded glove, pointing it at Jeez.

"I know who you are. Stay away," he said.

"Damien, your fate is sealed. Let her go," Jeez directed.

"No way. This woman will fetch a good price on the market in Megiddo," Damien responded.

"Let her go."

Damien laughed and spurred his horse on. The others followed. The woman turned to look at Tom and Jeez as she rode off. Moments later the four horsemen and their prisoner disappeared out of sight down the walkway.

∞

The hairs on Tom's neck stood up. "Who is Damien?

"Damien is the illegitimate son of Aristobulus IV, who enjoys protection of the Herodians." Jeez replied.

"What about the others?"

Jeez said, "All those auxiliaries report to the centurion who hired my father to install a *mikveh*, a ritual bath, in his home after he became a God-fearer. They have kidnapped the centurion's daughter, Mary Magdalene, and were riding his horses."

"Auxiliaries? Centurion? Horses? I'm confused. Where am I?"

"Never mind. Follow me." Jeez turned and walked up the hill.

One hundred paces later, the walkway veered left and a city of square, stone houses came into view. On the top of the hill, one of the houses burned with heavy smoke. On seeing this fire, Jeez began to run with Tom close behind him. At this point, Tom realized that he also wore a robe and sandals, and as was—running was awkward and laborious with the fabric hindering his stride.

Chapter Three

When Jeez reached the centurion's house, Tom caught up to him, stopped, and doubled over trying to catch his breath. Jeez stood straight, watching the burning house collapse into itself with a pained look. The fire had begun to die down with smoke and steam being more evident as neighbors threw buckets of water on the burning debris. The stench of burning flesh hung in the air.

"Tom, what strikes you as strange about this house?" Jeez asked.

"Other than it is burning down?" Tom responded.

"This is a big house with an interior court yard and many rooms. With a fire raging, why are the doors all shut?" Jeez asked.

"Huh? What are you saying?" Tom asked.

"People running out of a burning building don't stop to shut doors. No one escaped this fire and ran out," Jeez said.

"Were they sleeping when the fire began?" Tom

asked.

"No. People would normally have been up and about for at least a couple of hours preparing meals and doing household chores to avoid the heat of the day," Jeez explained.

"Are you suggesting that this fire was no accident?" Tom asked.

Jeez just turned and looked at Tom with tears running down his cheeks.

∞

The crowd of neighbors and other spectators parted as a contingent of Roman soldiers lead by a young Tribune Claudius, hurried down the street. The tribune stopped short of the smoldering ruins, turned, and held up his hand to address the crowd in front of Jeez and Tom.

"Whose household is this?" the tribune asked.

"This house belongs to the Centurion Augustine," Jeez responded.

"Augustine? How do you know this?"

"My father and I had been contracted to add a bath to the house."

The tribune looked at Jeez, "How did this fire start?"

"No idea. I have just returned from two days' break in Nazareth."

"Hmm. Come with me. Let's have a look. Let me know if anything looks out of place," the tribune directed his soldiers to clear a path through the rubble.

Jeez and Tom followed the tribune silently into the household, being careful to avoid stepping on smoldering embers. Inside the rooms, the walls and remaining furniture were blackened. The burned bodies of family members and slaves rested on the ledges in the stone walls where they normally slept. What was left of support beams from the floors of upper-story rooms lay in the rooms below. Containers and other clay vessels that held food and other supplies were smashed on the floor away from where they normally rested, out of keeping with simply fire damage.

The stable appeared untouched by fire, but the centurion's four horses and donkey were missing. In the ledges in the stable where Jeez and his father normally slept, Jospeh lay there with his throat cut. Jeez points to him.

"Tribune, this, this is my father," Jeez said with tears streaming down his face, turning away but still pointing. Tom embraces him tightly.

"He was clearly murdered, which suggests that the fire was intended to cover up even greater crimes," the tribune said.

"Yes. I know now who did this."

"Tell me. Tell me quickly."

"My friend, Tom, and I witnessed Damien and his crew riding four horses down the hill out of the city earlier this morning that belonged to the centurion, and they had the centurion's daughter, Mary Magdalene, bound on a donkey being led behind them."

"Are you sure?"

"I demanded that they release the daughter, but Damien threatened me with his sword and bragged that they were headed to sell her on the slave market in Megiddo."

"Your story makes sense. Megiddo is one route

to Sebastian, where they were recruited," Claudius explained.

"Centurion Augustine was a good man. Why would they target him and his family for murder?" Jeez asked.

"Unclear, but Governor Antipas recently ordered these men publicly scourged for extorting money from merchants who he had hired. Augustine discovered their crime and oversaw their punishment just before I arrived in Sepphoris. Perhaps, they could not bear the shame and sought revenge," Claudius replied.

"What will be done?" Jeez asked.

"You and your friend are witnesses to this crime and must accompany me in bringing these criminals to justice," Claudius directed.

"What about my father?" Jeez asked.

"You're from Nazareth, right? My soldiers will take your father's body back to Nazareth for burial and report on your whereabouts to your family. I will have my soldiers take your father's body back to Nazareth for burial and report on your whereabouts to your family."

"Thank you, tribune. My mother would surely worry."

"Now, we ride to Megiddo."

Chapter Four

Tom watched as the tribune ordered his men to fetch horses. A covered cart was prepared to transport his witnesses, carry provisions for the journey, and a few military contingencies, including several *hastas, gladii,* and shields. A day long trip to Megiddo in the blazing sun could be challenging for both man and beast.

While Tom stood waiting with Jeez, he asked, "How come you speak English with me and Greek with Claudius, while everyone else speaks another language?"

"I have a talent for languages. Everyone here speaks Aramaic, but business gets done in Greek. In Megiddo, you'll run into Parthian traders who primarily speak Persian. Among themselves, the Romans speak Latin, and the Jewish clergy speak Hebrew. English is a novelty around here," Jeez smiled.

"Are you a local translator?" Tom asked.

"Words are important. If you want to reach

hearts, you need to speak the heart's language," Jeez responded.

∞

As preparations continued, Jeez took Tom by the arm and walked over to speak with the tribune.

"Tribune, may I have a word?" Jeez asked.

"Be brief."

"Are you certain that the Sebastian auxiliaries were motivated by revenge? Soldiers are no stranger to discipline. Their crime seems disproportionate to the offense, even provocative. Why would they willingly disclose their escape route to Megiddo, knowing it would be reported?"

"Let's think about this a minute. I see two possible explanations for their disclosure if their real goal is to return to Sebastian," the tribune said.

"I like your thinking. Megiddo is the long route to Sebastian. The more direct route is through Nazareth and Jezreel," Jeez said.

"Exactly. Megiddo may be a diversion. Jezreel is also the winter headquarters of the Herodias family and their entourage. They have a palace next to the fortress. If these criminals rode directly to Jezreel, they could recruit comrades to help ambush us if we went to Megiddo, discovered our error, and traveled down the Jezreel Valley to Jezreel to catch up to them. We would be in plain sight for most of the trip, so they would see us coming," the Tribute said.

"Is this a trap?" Jeez asked.

"I have no idea, but I do know that Prefect Coponius would love to have an excuse to expand his domain to include Galilee. What do you suppose would happen if one of his tribunes were suspiciously killed by Galilean bandits while under Governor Antipas' protection?" the tribune asked.

"Two can play that game. If you take soldiers immediately to Jezreel, they won't have time to prepare a reception. If they first go to Megiddo, you can be the one to spring the trap," Tom said.

"The only problem is that I need Mary Magdalene as a witness to the crimes in Sepphoris. If she gets sold in the Megiddo slave market, you and your friend,

Tom, can only provide circumstantial evidence," the tribune said.

"Knowing her value as a witness, the Megiddo slave market is special because of the presence of Parthian traders who will whisk her far away from local courts," Jeez observed.

"Okay. Here's what we'll do. I will have you accompany Centurion Marcellus to Megiddo, while I take ten men to Jezreel. If you redeem Mary Magdalene, bring her to Jezreel. If I find no evidence of these criminals in Jezreel, I will come to Megiddo," the tribune said.

"What if Damien and his crew have traveled the Grand Trunk Road along the coast on to Sebastian?" Jeez asked.

"Then follow them to Sebastian."

As Tom watched, an auxiliary walked up leading the tribune's mount. The tribune conferred with Centurion Marcellus and gave him several gold coins. Then, he mounted his horse, issued orders to his men, and rode off.

The centurion walked over and called the cart driver to come up. Tom climbed aboard with Jeez, and they rolled off down the road out of Sepphoris. The centurion then mounted his horse and took the lead.

∞

At the base of Sepphoris hill, the tribune and his men kept riding towards Nazareth, while the centurion and the cart turned right on the road to Megiddo. As Tom watched, the tribune soon disappeared in the distance.

Clop, clop, clop. Riding along in the cart, Tom turned to Jeez and asked, "Are you as nervous as I am that we're no longer in the company of Tribune Claudius and his men?"

"Claudius is young for a tribune and I will miss his company. However, we're not alone. God is with us," Jeez said.

"You prefer God's presence to a tribune and ten soldiers?" Tom asked.

"You don't know Centurion Marcellus," Jeez

responded, avoiding the question.

"That guy?" Tom looked at the centurion.

"That guy! In his youth, Centurion Marcellus managed the security detail for Herod the Great. He is a quiet man, but on one occasion, he struck down four assassins single-handedly."

"Four assassins?"

"Yes. Four of the nastiest, best-trained killers in the known world. Because of his skill and valor, the Romans recruited and promoted him to the centurion rank along with giving him citizenship—something rare indeed. His nickname among the Romans is Hercules. Jewish soldiers call him Samson," Jeez responded.

Tom turned and stared at the centurion.

"We're going to be fine."

∞

Later in the morning, Tom looked down the hill to the Valley of Jezreel. The city of Megiddo could be seen across the valley. The centurion stopped, dismounted his horse, and took a water break, sitting under the last stone pine before the treeless valley below. Jeez and Tom joined him sitting under the tree.

Tom turned to Jeez. "Do you think that the world will come to an end with a battle at Megiddo?"

"Megiddo has the smell of death. King Saul died near there. The righteous King Josiah—the hope of Israel—was also killed in a battle near there," Jeez responded.

"Why do good men have to die?"

"Death is a divine curse brought about by Adam's sin."

"I don't need theology." Tom paused. "Why don't you just answer my questions?"

"Some questions have no answers. For others, you're not ready."

"Jeez, I do not understand you. We found your father, Joseph, murdered this morning and you have said nothing."

Jeez looked up, his eyes unblinking. "Death is outside my experience and I'm sad but do not understand it. In any case, how can I *sit shiva* with my mother while my father's killers roam free and threaten Mary Magdalene with a life of bondage?"

"I don't understand death either. I lost my father. I feel empty and alone without words to explain any of it," Tom reached out and put his hand on Jeez's shoulder.

Now rested, Marcellus stood, put on his helmet and peered over the valley. He pointed and said, "Look. There are ridders halfway across the valley traveling towards Megiddo."

Tom and Jeez jumped to their feet and strained to see the riders.

"I count four horses and donkey," Tom whispered to Jeez.

"You're right. It must be them," Jeez said.

"Let's go," Marcellus directed.

ACT TWO

Chapter 5

It was mid-afternoon, Tom followed Jeez in climbing into the cart. As the driver took his seat, Marcellus turned and walked his horse alongside the cart.

"I know that you and your friend are not soldiers, but I need you to do something for me," Marcellus said.

"Sure. Anything," Jeez responded.

"Grab one of the *hastas*—Roman spears—in the cart and keep watch as we journey through the tall grass in the valley. Lion prides love to use tall grass to camouflage their ambushes. A few seconds is all one has to defend oneself during an attack," Marcellus explained.

White-faced, Tom and Jeez both picked up *hastas* and gaze into the tall grass along the trail.

"Thanks for the warning," Jeez said.

"We're in this together. The Jezreel valley is famous for lion attacks," Marcellus continued.

"Centurion, you're scaring me," Tom said.

"A little fear goes a long way around here. Prides

have been famous for circling Megiddo at night and waking the residents with their hungry roars. Murderers are occasionally sentenced to be locked out of the city naked and barefoot at dusk. We won't be safe until we enter the city gates," Marcellus reported.

When he finished speaking, Marcellus drew his sword, spurred his horse forward, and signaled the cart driver to follow him. Tom positioned himself on one side of the cart with a death grip on his *hasta* as the cart rolled down the hill. Jeez watched the other side.

∞

As Tom surveyed the grassy landscape broken only by an occasional rock formation or stand of trees, he turned to Jeez. "How come I understood and could speak with Marcellus?"

"Interesting question. It seems that you're learning Greek!" Jeez replied.

"Greek? I don't understand," Tom said.

"God equips those he calls," Jeez responded.

∞

Midway through the Jezreel Valley east of

Megiddo in the heat of the day, Tom noticed a gaggle of vultures circling overhead near a dried-out riverbed and pointed it out to Jeez.

"Those vultures circling up ahead suggest a recent lion kill. The pride is likely still there," Tom reported.

Jeez tapped the cart driver on the shoulder and pointed to the vultures. The driver immediately repeated the warning to Marcellus.

"I noticed," Marcellus responded. "Let's go around it—quietly. No shouting."

Marcellus led his horse and the cart off the trail. He headed south several hundred meters to avoid the vultures and keep the noise of the cart wheels out of earshot. Once clear of the vultures, he turned east again, crossed the riverbed, then headed north to return to the road east to Megiddo.

"I wonder who or what was ambushed by the lion pride back there?" Tom said to Jeez.

"Perhaps we'll learn in Megiddo," Jeez answered.

As they got within a mile of Megiddo, Tom observed the four soldiers on horseback leaving Megiddo by the south road. "Where is Mary Magdalene?" Tom asked.

"They must have sold her in the slave market," Jeez responded.

∞

Marcellus turned his horse around, approached the cart, and dismounted. "My orders are to pursue the criminals. I need you to continue to Megiddo and redeem Mary Magdalene from whoever purchased her and escort her safely back to Sepphoris. Step down from the cart and stand in front of me," Marcellus said.

Jeez and Tom got out of the cart and stood in front of Marcellus.

"State your names." Marcellus asked.

"Jeez," Jeez said.

"Tom," Tom said.

"Hold up your right hands."

Jeez and Tom raised their right hands.

"Jeez and Tom. I deputize you as deputy auxiliaries in the name of the Emperor Augustus. Do you accept this commission?"

Tom looked at Jeez.

"We do."

Marcellus reached into the cart and retrieved two *gladii,* Roman swords with matching scabbards and belts.

"These *gladii* are the symbol of your office. You'll receive a denarius for each day of service." Tom and Jeez took the *gladii* from Marcellus. "Wear the *gladius* under your cloaks and do not display them to anyone unless a need arises. Keep a low profile. Megiddo is a dangerous place under the best of circumstances," Marcellus said.

Marcellus handed backpacks to Jeez and Tom, and two gold coins to Jeez. "The coins should be enough to redeem Mary Magdalene. These backpacks contain three days rations and water. You also will need *hastas* to defend yourself from wild animals and brigands. If you succeed in your mission, we can talk about joining the Sepphoris cohort permanently when you return."

Marcellus then turned, mounted his horse, and led the cart off towards the south road after the soldiers. Soon the clop, clop of the cart and pounding hooves faded in the distance.

Jeez opened his hand to look at the gold coins, amazed at what had just transpired.

"Marcellus obviously trusts you," Tom observed.

"Let's go redeem Mary Magdalene."

Tom and Jeez put on their backpacks, strapped on their swords, and hike for the front gate of Megiddo using their *hastas* as walking sticks.

Chapter Six

As Tom and Jeez approached the east Megiddo city gate late in the afternoon, a guard and a tax collector stopped them.

"What is your business in Megiddo?" the guard shouted over the commotion in the city market that is just beyond the gate.

"We're here on official business from the Sepphoris cohort," Jeez pulled back his cloak to reveal his *gladius*.

"Could you be more specific?" the guard insisted.

"A young female witness to a murder in Sepphoris has been sold on the slave market here in Megiddo. We've been sent to redeem her and escort her back to Sepphoris," Jeez responded.

"I believe that I know the girl you seek." The guard pointed to a group of men wearing trousers instead of robes. "Those Parthian traders on the other side of market purchased her within the hour." He waved Tom and Jeez through the gate.

Once inside the city, Tom pulls Jeez aside. "I thought that slavery among Hebrews, especially women, was banned by the law of Moses."

"You're right, but the enforcement of the ban weakens the further you travel away from Jerusalem." Jeez said.

"Hmm. Officials are no doubt receiving bribes to look the other way." Tom suggested.

"Megiddo is important in this trade because the buyers are foreigners who transport slaves purchased to distant lands, often within a single day." Jeez said.

∞

Tom saw seven Parthians lead prisoners bound with leather straps. Several rode white horses.

The leader of the group, an older man with a white silk shirt and matching turban, tried without success to comfort a young man bound by his hands and feet. The young man struggled and raged incoherently.

Jeez walked back to the guard at the gate and

asked, "What is wrong with this young man?"

"A lion mauled the leader's son yesterday down by the riverbank before archers could kill it. Gravely wounded, the son's flesh has festered, and he has lost his mind. His father is beside himself with grief," the guard explained.

Jeez walked back to Tom. He handed him his *hasta* and his *gladius*. "These weapons are of no use in the battle that I must fight," Jeez responded as he walked towards the Parthians.

As he drew near to the stretcher, the young man called out in the Persian language, "What do you have to do with me, Jesus of Nazareth?"

The father, the leader of the Parthians, looked up and saw Jeez.

"In the name of the God who created heaven and earth, come out of him," Jeez commanded in the Persian language.

The young man tried to jump, let out a shriek, and became quiet. Startled, the father looked at his son and could see that the son's fever had subsided, and his wounds had healed. His son opened his eyes as if waking from a deep sleep and smiled at his father. The father hugged his son and began to cry. Then he turned to Jeez and asked, "What do you want from us?"

"I was sent to redeem a young slave woman from Sepphoris," Jeez responded.

"Is that the woman?" The father pointed to Mary Magdalene.

"Yes," Jeez responded.

The father turned to his men and said, "Release the woman to this man."

"A blessing on your house and family from the Lord Almighty, Arash Anahita, son of Hawar, follower of *Ahura Mazda*."

Hearing his name and his god, the father looked at Jeez amazed, "My father was a Magi who visited this land more than ten years ago. He cautioned me to keep an eye out for a *Saoshyant*, born King of the Jews. Are you this *Saoshyant*?" Arash asked.

"Can a compass point to itself? Can one find meaning in the vacuum of self?" Jeez asked.

Arash's jaw dropped. "We do not contemplate riddles, mysteries, and mantras, like princes who use drugs, hooks, and chains to confuse and dominate weak minds. We only practice good thoughts, good words, and good deeds."

"I'm just the son of a carpenter," Jeez shrugged.

"Not everyone with a mustache is your father," Arash responded.

Jeez smiled, turned, and walked away.

Jeez and Mary Magdalene returned to the gate where Tom was standing and together they left the city.

∞

Exiting the east gate in early evening, Tom observed. "We've got a problem. While you were in the market retrieving Mary Magdalene, a dozen or so sketchy characters took an interest in you. We may be followed by brigands if we travel directly to Sepphoris."

"You forget the lions. They ambush and prefer to hunt at night. It's a rookie mistake to travel through their territory at night," Jeez said.

"Lions?" Mary Magdalene repeated. She turns to Tom, looking disturbed.

"Lions ambushed the Parthians close to Megiddo along the riverbank. The vultures that we saw earlier today must have marked the spot," Jeez reported.

"What if we hurried around to Megiddo's south gate before dark so the brigands don't see us? It's safer in the city at night," Tom suggested.

Mary Magdalene nodded with agreement. "I like that idea. Let's run before they see us."

Tom looked back at the gate to see if the brigands were watching, which they were not.

"Run. Run," Mary Magdalene repeated.

They ran around the city along the wall and slide into the south gate just before it is closed for the night. Jeez said, "The brigands must have known better than to follow us out of the city in the evening. In the morning, let's head south to Jezreel just to be sure. Maybe we can find a caravan to travel with."

"Great idea. Perhaps we'll catch up to Marcellus and Tribune Claudius in Jezreel," Tom said.

"Works for me," Mary Magdalene affirmed.

∞

Mary Magdalene stopped one of the local women, "Where do travelers spend the night?"

"Most travelers congregate around the entrance to the steps to the well at night where the watchmen keep an eye on them," the woman responded, looking anxious.

Sensing that woman wanted to say something else, Mary Magdalene pushed on, "Do you have something else to add?"

Pointing to the well's entrance, the woman continued, "The Megiddo well is a marvel of qanat engineering, much like Hezekiah's Tunnel in Jerusalem. It provides water in season and out, keeping the city safe in times of siege. This is why watchmen are assigned to guard it. Our enemies would love to poison our well."

"What is *qanat* engineering?" Tom asked.

"*Qanat* is a Semitic word than means conduit. It is a series of rock channels that allow spring water to flow naturally from a well to another location, developed by the Persians," the woman responded.

"This is amazing," Mary Magdalene said.

"Even under guard, one must sleep with one eye open, because thieves prey on travelers. It is better to fetch some water and to sleep by the south gate under the night watchman's eyes. There is even a bed pan there, should the need arise," the woman said.

"Who thought to make a bed pan available?" Mary Magdalene asked.

"The priests insist that we bury our sewage outside the city. The fields outside are very fertile! The bed pans are provided to encourage visitors who are not from here to honor our purity laws," the woman reported.

Mary Magdalene looked worriedly at Jeez and Tom.

"Let's sleep by the south gate." Jeez suggested.

"We have some dried fruit and bread in the backpacks. We can fill our gourds before setting out in the morning," Tom said.

Chapter Seven

Monday morning, Tom, Mary Magdalene, and Jeez woke before sunrise, startled by the roaring of hungry lions who prowled around the city walls angry because they could not get in. The lions departed at sunrise as archers fired on them from the city walls, killing one. With no caravans scheduled for the morning, the three travelers breakfasted on dried fruit and departed Megiddo with the opening of the city gates on the south road to Jezreel.

After they traveled out of sight of Megiddo, Jeez asked Mary Magdalene, "Tell me about the death of my father?"

"There is not much to tell," Mary Magdalene replied. "I woke with a knife at my throat. Everyone's throat had already been cut," Mary Magdalene's voice cracked as she spoke.

Tom walked over and embraced Mary Magdalene.

"Why did they do this?" Jeez asked.

"No idea. I was gagged, bound, and set on a

donkey without a word. After that they set fire to the house, and we rode away. Within minutes of all this, I saw you and Tom on the road," Mary Magdalene said, breaking away from Tom.

"Tribune Claudius said that the soldiers had been scourged for extorting money from merchants that Governor Antipas had hired. Did you witness it?" Jeez inquired.

"I heard about the scourging, but did not witness it," Mary Magdalene whispered.

∞

Mary Magdalene exchanged glances with Tom.

"Are you okay? Tom asked, but she looked down and did not respond. "You had a rough day yesterday, between the murders, the trip to Megiddo, and the slave market."

"I am cursed with the loss of two families—my birth family and now my adopted family. What is to become of me?"

"That is a lot of trauma for anyone to deal with." Tom observed. "But you have to understand that none of this is your fault."

"I do understand mentally, but my heart is broken and I cannot help but feel guilty for having survived."

"Survivor guilt is perfectly normal. Obviously, God is not done with you—you are alive for a reason. Pray to God and ask him to reveal to you why he has offered you such an important blessing."

"Blessing?"

"Life is itself a blessing, an ongoing reason to give thanks to God."

Jeez stopped and looked at Mary Magdalene.

"Forgive me for bringing all this up again," Jeez said.

Mary Magdalene turned to look at him.

"Don't worry about it," she said.

∞

For the next two hours, Tom, Mary Magdalene, and Jeez hiked the south road to Jezreel in silence and without incident. They limped with sore feet and drank the last of their water. As they approached Jezreel mid-morning, vultures circled the road ahead of them. Tom looked at Jeez with apprehension and they leave the road to avoid the vultures.

"What is it?" Mary Magdalene asked.

"Yesterday, we saw vultures circling where lions attacked the Parthians. This could be another lion ambush ahead," Tom responded.

At a distance, they walked by the site of the circling vultures. Then, Jeez stopped and pointed. "Look. It is Marcellus and the cart driver." They returned to the road.

"Are they okay?" Tom asked.

"Marcellus has his arms crossed. They look as though they have been waiting for us," Jeez answered.

∞

Drawing near to the site, Tom could see wild dogs gnawing on bloody bones and fighting off vultures that wanted their share of the carcasses. By the time they grew closer, only skulls, feet, and hands remain, as had been reported of Queen Jezebel who died near this spot hundreds of years earlier. The smell is overwhelming, and flies are everywhere. Off to the side, the driver stowed Roman armor, helmets, and *gladii* in his cart. Marcellus' horse was tied to the cart so he walked over to meet Tom, Jeez, and Mary Magdalene.

"I see that you succeeded in your mission. I have saved armor and helmets for your use," Marcellus signaled to the cart driver to retrieve these items.

Seeing the armor and realizing what had just happened, Mary Magdalene covered her mouth with her hand and looked away.

"Thank you, centurion. Because my father has been murdered, I must care for my mother and family. An auxiliary's pay will be most helpful," Jeez said.

"Keep in mind that Roman citizenship requires twenty-five years' service. Was there change from the redemption?" Marcellus asked.

Jeez handed Marcellus the two gold coins that he had been given.

Marcellus looked incredulous. "What? How did you redeem the girl?"

"I spoke to the leader of the Parthian slave traders, and he released her," Jeez responded.

Marcellus looked puzzled, then relaxed.

"Good. We no longer need witnesses," Marcellus said.

"How come?" Jeez asked.

"Tribune Claudius Lysias and his men were waiting for Damien and his crew, and captured them here. When they were searched, they found centurion Augustine's sword and his wife's jewelry in their possession. Angry, the tribune found them guilty of desertion and sentenced them to decimation," Marcellus reported.

"Decimation? I thought that it had been outlawed," Jeez said.

"Not in extreme cases like this one, where desertion is compounded with theft and murder," Marcellus replied.

"What is decimation?" Tom asked.

"Decimation is when the deserter is beaten to death by ten of his fellow soldiers. Its cruelty served as an example to others to remain loyal," Jeez responded.

Mary Magdalene gasped.

"If you no longer need witnesses, what will become of Mary Magdalene? She has no family," Jeez looked at her.

"You redeemed her. She is your problem," Marcellus responded.

"With my father murdered, my mother is pregnant without a husband. She could use a daughter in Nazareth to help her get by while I serve in Sepphoris," Jeez said.

"Very well. We can drop Mary Magdalene off in Nazareth on our return to Sepphoris," Marcellus said.

Chapter Eight

Already almost noon, it's hot. They refilled their gourds from a spring near Jezreel and ate provisions from their backpacks.

Marcellus directed, "Okay, let's go."

Tom, Mary Magdalene, and Jeez passed around a gourd with water, got into the horse cart and departed with Marcellus on his horse in the lead. They lumbered past Jezreel into the highlands of Galilee towards Nazareth.

Time passed. Bored with the heat, dust, and long journey, as they approached Nazareth mid-afternoon, Tom turned to Mary Magdalene and asked, "I'm just curious. How did the soldiers pay for you in the Megiddo slave market?"

Mary Magdalene looked away, embarrassed. "Do you always get right to the point? The Parthians gave the soldiers four old, brown horses."

Startled, Tom turned to look at Jeez. "Four brown horses? Damien has played us! The auxiliaries traveling to Jezreel were a diversion."

Jeez shouted to Marcellus, "Centurion, when the tribune and his men captured the criminals, what color horses were they riding?"

"The tribune collected four brown horses from the criminals and sent them back to Sepphoris," Marcellus shouted back.

Jeez turned to Tom and whispered, "Tribune Claudius decimated the wrong soldiers."

Marcellus turned his horse around, the horse jumped, and came alongside of the cart. "Why did you ask about the horses?"

"Tom suggested that the auxiliaries captured in front of Jezreel may have been a diversion. The murderers sold Mary Magdalene for four brown horses and may have sent them with other soldiers to Jezreel along with the centurion's sword and jewelry," Jeez explained.

"Where are Damien and the other criminals?" Marcellus asked.

"Not clear. They may have taken the Grand Trunk Road north out of Megiddo towards Caesarea along the coast of the *Yam Gadol* or Great Sea, instead of the easier central route through Jezreel as we assumed," Jeez responded.

"If that is true, we can beat them to Sebastian by at least a day by taking the central route," Marcellus said.

"Could we drop off Mary Magdalene in Nazareth and leave in the morning?" Jeez asked.

"We need to stop in Nazareth of necessity. We need to pick up some horses for you and Tom in Nazareth, and send the cart back to Sepphoris for reinforcements," Marcellus responded.

"Reinforcements are good. Tom and I are not expert horsemen and have no military training. How can we support you in arresting four seasoned soldiers?" Jeez observed.

"You need only look the part. We'll have the element of surprise on our side because of Tom's astute observations. They also know my history. Their own fear will deliver them into our hands," Marcellus responded.

∞

At mid-afternoon, cart and horse arrived at the outskirts of Nazareth. The travelers are sweaty, tired. and hungry. Word quickly spread that the carpenter's son was now an auxiliary and had arrived with a centurion, another soldier, and a young woman. A small crowd gathered around them as they approached Jeez's family home. Jeez's mother, Mary, stood outside to greet them, obviously pregnant, with several neighbor women. Jeez jumped out of the cart and ran to meet her.

"Mother!" Jeez shouted. He then embraced her and began to cry.

Without a word, Marcellus dismounted, took off his helmet, and placed it under his arm. The cart driver got down from his seat and held his horse. Tom and Mary Magdalene climbed down from the cart.

Realizing that he wasn't alone, Jeez wiped the tears from his eyes and began introductions.

"Mother, this is Centurion Marcellus, who led us in pursuing father's murderers."

"Thank you for your courage and devotion to duty," Mary told Marcellus, who bowed.

Jeez pointed to Tom. "This my friend Tom," Tom smiled.

Jeez motioned with his hand for Mary Magdalene to approach.

"Mother, behold your daughter," he said.

"Mary, behold your mother," he continued.

Mary Magdalene ran over and hugged Mary.

After a few minutes of family bonding, Mary called over the neighbor women and spoke with them briefly. Then she addressed her guests, "You must all be tired from the journey. Please sit under the canopy here on our porch. Enjoy some wine while I prepare some food."

∞

While Marcellus, Tom, Mary Magdalene, and the driver relaxed and ate, Mary took Jeez aside.

"Who is this woman that you have brought home?" Mary asked.

"Mary Magdalene is an orphan who needs you

as much as you need her," Jeez responded.

"You know what I mean," Mary quipped.

"Her family in Magdala perished in a pandemic three years ago, and Centurion Augustine adopted her as a daughter. When the criminals murdered Father and her family, she was kidnapped and sold on the slave market in Megiddo, where I redeemed her from Parthian traders," Jeez responded.

"So, she has been traumatized?" Mary inquired.

"She is a strong, resilient woman. With Father dead and my working as a soldier, in my absence she can be the daughter that you have always wanted," Jeez explained.

"Do you think that I'm helpless?" Mary asked.

Jeez looks at Mary with a great sadness. "No, Mom. With Joseph dead and you with child, I worry about you."

"Perhaps, she would make you a good Jewish wife?" Mary mused.

Jeez stiffened and looked off in the distance. "No, Mom. Today, I'm a soldier caring for his family.

Tomorrow, I must take another role," Looking restless, he asked, "Show me father's grave before I go."

"Why do you ask? You already know the place. Take your friend Tom with you," Mary said.

∞

Marcellus took the cart driver aside and quietly directed him. "In the morning, travel back to Sepphoris and report to Tribune Claudius about Jezreel and our plans to arrest the criminals in Sebastian."

"Claudius won't be happy," the driver opined. "He decimated the wrong soldiers and could face discipline."

"If you value your life, tell Claudius privately and no one else," Marcellus responded.

The driver looked at Marcellus as if he had seen a ghost, but said nothing.

∞

Jeez returned to the porch canopy where everybody ate flat bread, dried fish, raisins, and olives prepared by the neighborhood women. Jeez greeted everyone but nodded at Tom and motioned with his finger for him to come with him.

"Let's go for a walk," Jeez said.

"You look tired. What's up?" Tom asked.

Jeez put his arm around Tom as he walked through the village to a garden. "Grief is exhausting. The Jewish custom is to *sit shiva,* which means that family and friends come to the grieving person's house and just sit with them for seven days without a word."

"We have had no silence, no rest, not even regular meals," Tom remarked. "We've both aged in the brief time we have been together."

"For sure. We have both had to grow up quickly with our fathers' passing." Jeez observed. "I brought you here because I knew that you would understand my pain."

"I'm not sure that I understand, but how can we *sit shiva* when grief overwhelms us?" Tom responded as they walked.

Jeez pointed to a garden, bordered with towering columns of white flowers, but otherwise unadorned. "The white squill is planted around graveyards throughout Israel, because it is poisonous to rats that eagerly eat it and die."

In spite of the dry, rocky soil, Tom could see a new gravesite.

Jeez fell to his knees, looked up, and said, "May the Lord grant my father mercy on the day of judgment."

Tom fell to his knees next to him and said, "Amen. And may the Lord grant us his presence and strength on that day."

Jeez cried. Tom put his arm around him and they sobbed together.

∞

As it grew dark, Mary Magdalene came to the graveyard, where she found Jeez and Tom weeping on their knees. She threw her arms around the two and sobbed with them. Time passed.

"Your mother wants you to return and eat something." Jeez's thin frame became more obvious as he stood. "Marcellus says that you must travel early in the morning," Mary Magdalene told them.

"Yes, of course," Jeez responded.

Tom got up silently and helped Jeez to his feet. They walk back to the house.

Jeez turned to Mary Magdalene and asked, "How are you doing?"

"I'm still numb. My grief is most acute when I am tired," she said.

"When you're ready, turn your pain over to God. It is too much to bear on your own. Let him bear it for you," Jeez said.

Mary Magdalene smiled and hugged him.

∞

After they returned home, Mary invited her male guests to sleep on woven mats on the roof. Because the day had been hot and the weather still pleasant, everyone climbed up a ladder to the roof and settled in to relax stargazing at Cassiopeia, Ursa Major, and the North Star after a long day.

Marcellus reminded Tom and Jeez, "I bought horses for you while you were away."

"Thank you. I won't miss the bumpy ride of the

horse cart," Tom commented.

"Ha. The bumps didn't wake you. You'll miss snoring on the horse," Jeez joked.

"Actually, you'll learn to sleep on horseback. Just be sure to lean forward, not backward," Marcellus paused. "Before I forget. I asked Mary to prepare breakfast early, as we need to leave before sunrise to avoid the heat of the day, especially as we cross the Jezreel Valley," Marcellus commented.

"You think of everything," Tom responded.

"See you in the morning," Jeez said.

∞

In the dead of the night, Marcellus screamed in pain and rolled around. Tom and Jeez wake anxiously.

"What's happening?" Tom called out in the dark, terrified.

Marcellus threshed around in the dark and screamed again.

"Mother, bring a torch," Jeez shouted.

Marcellus continued flailing around.

An eternity passes. Mary climbed up the ladder

to the roof with a torch. When its light shown on the roof, Jeez pointed to a yellow-greenish scorpion the size of a shoe close to Marcellus and poised to strike again. Tom picked up a bedpan, emptied its contents off the side of the roof, and smashed the scorpion.

Marcellus lay shuddering, his hands balled up, and his teeth clinched. Jeez placed his hand on Marcellus' shoulder and closed his eyes. His lips moved, but he said nothing. Marcellus relaxed. Jeez put a sheet over him and Marcellus slept.

"What just happened?" Tom asked.

Smelling the former contents of the bedpan, Mary held her nose and retreated down the ladder.

"Never mind," Jeez laid down, rolled over, pulled a sheet over his shoulder, and went back to sleep.

Tom laid back down, but sleep evaded him most of the night.

∞

Before the sun broke over the horizon on Tuesday morning, Tom dreamed that he was a star player on his school's football team being chased down the field by defenders and had just scored the winning goal. The stadium crowd went wild and were cheering his victory along with his mother and father. He was excited. When he opened his eyes, he only saw a night sky and stars twinkling. The dream was over and his ears focused on sounds coming from the chicken coop across the street. He missed the cheerleaders in the dream, led by his friend Maddie.

"Tom, are you awake?" Jeez asked.

"What was your clue?" Tom responded.

While Tom and Jeez talked, Marcellus got up, oblivious to what transpired during the night. With great difficulty, he made his way down the ladder to the porch where breakfast called his name.

Still on the roof, Tom asked, "May I ask a question?"

"What's on your mind?" Jeez responded.

"Do you ever feel invisible?" Tom asked.

"What do you mean?" Jeez responded.

"Every time you do something remarkable; you

blow it off with your stock phrase—Never mind."

"What's your point?" Jeez asked.

"When you cut me off with your stock phrase, I feel like my opinions don't matter. Actually, I feel that way a lot," Tom said.

Silent for a moment, Jeez demurred, "Your opinions do matter. I will try to listen better," he paused. "Are you hungry? We have big day ahead."

"Sure. Lead on, but tell me one thing, should I be afraid to fall asleep? I feel like I have been dropped into a bygone world full of ghosts from the past." Tom said.

"Fear not, for I am with you always," Jeez responded.

ACT THREE

Chapter Nine

Tom ate breakfast with the other travelers under the canopy on the porch.

Marcellus struggled to talk, as the effects of the scorpion attack lingered. "I need to return to Sepphoris and may even need to ride in the cart."

Jeez glanced at Tom, "What about Damien?"

Tom looked worried.

"You'll need to lead the chase without me. Tribune Claudius will catch up to you on the Ridge Road to Sebastian," Marcellus advised.

"I've never been there," Jeez responded.

Tom stood up shaken.

Mary Magdalene interrupted, "I know the route. I traveled there with the family only last spring."

Tom stares at Mary Magdalene.

"You're needed here," Jeez replied.

"I can manage on my own for a few weeks," Mary interjected.

"You can take my horse. It's a Numidian from North Africa. Dressed as an auxiliary with your hair tucked under your helmet, no one will know you're a woman," Marcellus offered.

"I'll do whatever it takes to see Damien brought to justice," Mary Magdalene chimed in.

Tom turned to look at Jeez with a sense of astonishment.

"Jeez, lend me a hand." With his help, Marcellus walked over to the cart and retrieved a *gladius* with matching scabbards and belt. He then motioned for Mary Magdalene to stand in front of him. "I deputize you as a deputy auxiliary in the name of the Emperor Augustus. Do you accept this commission?"

"I do," Mary Magdalene responded.

Marcellus handed her the *gladius*. "Get dressed. You need to leave immediately. While you're serving the emperor, your *nom de guerre* is Leo. No one should suspect you're anything but a *lethal* Roman auxiliary."

"Leo?" Mary Magdalene smiled, looking at Tom who suddenly realized that she was a spitting image of Maddie.

∞

While "Leo" went to change into her uniform, Tom sat by himself eating his breakfast and reflecting on the last conversation that he had with his father.

. "Dad, you don't need to take me to the youth group meeting this evening. Mom can take me," Tom headed for the door.

"Not to worry. I have to work late this evening and it's on my way—we can take the cruiser." His father grabbed his pistol, body armor, and police windbreaker, and headed toward the door.

"Okay." Tom walked out to the driveway and waited by the passenger's side of the car.

"Do you think that Maddie's parents can give you a ride home?" His dad unlocked the car doors and they got in.

"Sure. No problem." Tom buckled his seatbelt.

"What's the program about tonight?" His dad started the car.

"Beats me. I wasn't paying attention when they made the announcement."

"Hmm. Why not?"

"I'm not sure that youth group is for me. It seems too girly. They mostly want to read books, and discuss emotions and relationships. The only other guys in the group have parents working at the church."

"Rather play sports?"

"Maybe. I have been thinking about taking up soccer or going out for the cross-country team."

Dad pulled into the church parking lot, turned to Tom, and said, "Hang in there. You can do both. Make your peace with God and hang with people that can help you with that journey. Just pick a sport that doesn't practice on Sunday mornings."

"Thanks for the ride. Catch you later." As he closed the car door and his father waved, Tom's thoughts returned to breakfast under the canopy. He takes a bite of his breakfast.

∞

Jeez walked over and sat next to Tom, drawing him into being fully present.

"Can I ask you a question?" Tom asked.

"What's on your mind?"

"Your father and my father were both murdered. We never got to say goodbye to them. What would you say if you got the chance?"

"I don't know. What would you say?"

"I love you, Dad. That's what I would say."

"It doesn't sound like enough."

"It's not. We don't get to say all that we would want to. . . . Death is thief."

"How did you end up my spirit guide? Jeez paused. "Are you okay with pursuing Damien without Marcellus?"

"It depends on whether you believe that Tribune Claudius and his men will catch up with us on the road to Sebastian," Tom responded. "We cannot arrest Damien and his crew without serious help."

"Good point. I suspect that comment was designed to allay our fears. Earlier Claudius expressed concern that Prefect Coponius would love to have an excuse to expand his domain to include Galilee. Even for him, this could be a dangerous mission because it's outside his jurisdiction," Jeez observed.

"Do you think that Claudius may flinch at pursuing these criminals into the heart of Samaria?" Tom rephrased.

"The prefect could argue that Claudius allowed lawlessness to break out in Galilee, which would require a stronger hand be appointed in Sepphoris. Alternatively, that Claudius had exceeded his authority in pursuing criminals in Samaria," Jeez argued. "Consider what Copenius might argue if we were ambushed by these criminals in Samaria—"

"No proof of a crime for lack of witnesses?" Tom hinted.

"Exactly," Jeez said.

"No justice in an unjust time?" Tom summarized.

"One way or another, Copenius won't know who we are unless Claudius shows up to make introductions," Jeez noted.

"Perhaps, Marcellus can write out a warrant for the arrest of the criminals that we can carry to provide necessary introductions and authority," Tom suggested.

"You are truly your father's son," Jeez observed.

Tom looked at Jeez and smiled.

∞

Leo returned to the canopy in her auxiliary's armor. Tom looked up and clapped. Everyone present joined in.

"I see that we have a *lethal auxiliary* ready to lead the chase to Sebastian," Jeez announced.

"Marcellus, before we leave, we need one more thing. Could you write a warrant for the arrest of the four soldiers that we can present to Prefect Copernicus?" Tom asked.

Marcellus nodded. "Absolutely. Do we have parchment suitable for the task?"

"I will fetch some," Mary offered.

Mary returned with parchment, and Marcellus wrote out a warrant. Tom, Jeez, and Leo saddled their horses while the cart driver packed three days' provisions on a donkey. As soon as the warrant was written and signed, they mounted their horses and said their goodbyes.

“The trip to Sebastian is a long day on horseback. Bandits watch the road, but three auxiliaries keeping a steady pace on the Ridge Road are unlikely to be approached," Marcellus cautioned.

“What do we do about the night?” Jeez asked.

“Be on your guard at stops and the several taverns along the way. Seasoned soldiers slow the pace during the day, water the horses at every opportunity, and journey through the night to avoid ambush. You can rest once you enter the gated city at Sebastian," Marcellus said, handing Jeez a gold coin. They exchanged salutes, spurred their horses, and set off.

∞

Over the next couple hours, Leo led Tom and Jeez down the road to Jezreel where they stopped to water the horses. Afterwards, they cross the Jezreel valley.

“Why did Damien brandish his sword on the road to Sepphoris and blame you for what happened?”

Tom asked Jeez, provoking Leo to turn around in the saddle and give Jeez an inquisitive look.

"Hard to say. The rumor went around the household that Damien grew up near Gerasene with an abusive father. However, that rumor makes no sense, because he runs around repeating that he is the son of Aristobulus IV, an aristocrat who lived briefly in Sebastian. He joined the Sebastian cohort at a young age but later transferred to Sepphoris to escape his father's influence and control," Jeez responded.

"But why did he blame you?" Tom repeated.

"Running away from his problems became a pattern for Damien. He blamed others, especially God, for all his failures and weaknesses. He may be physically short, but he is long on attitude. His attitude about me—another of his victims—was no different."

"That sounds evil," Leo observed.

"It is hard to forgive someone like that," Tom said.

"Damien's cowardice makes him evil. His brilliance makes him dangerous," Jeez summarized.

∞

Once across the Jezreel valley, Leo pushed up the trail toward the ridge line with Tom and Jeez behind her. Not a word was spoken until around noon. The sun and heat is unrelenting.

"How are we going to arrest Damien and his squad? They outnumber us and are seasoned soldiers, while we're fit primarily for a costume party," Tom inquired.

"We'll need to present Marcellus' warrant to the tribune in Sebastian and request his assistance," Jeez responded.

"Tribune Marcus will defer any decision to Herodias whose response will be totally self-serving," Leo chimed in.

"Why do you say that? Tom asked.

"Marcus is a man-child who favors boys to women. He mostly worries about fashion and his public persona. Herodias is ambitious and believes that she should add Galilee to her personal domain. Damien and his squad were likely commissioned by

Herodias to stir up trouble and provide an excuse to depose Governor Antipas," Leo explained.

“How do you know all that?” Tom inquired.

Leo looked at Jeez who nodded.

“Centurion Augustine brought me to Sebastian ostensibly to serve as a handmaiden to Herodias during the summer while he traveled on further to Jerusalem. In reality, I was quietly commissioned by Governor Antipas to keep an eye on Herodias," Leo reported.

“You were a court spy?” Tom asked, sounding amused.

“You can't tell anyone," Leo pleaded.

"No wonder Marcellus was quick to embrace your role in this trip. He had confidence in you because he knew your true pedigree. Was Leo your handle?” Tom asked.

Leo smiled without a word.

∞

Leo led Tom and Jeez up a steep hill with the afternoon sun in their faces.

"We're approaching the ridge line that runs along the Jezreel Valley all the way from Megiddo. It is possible that Damien and his squad followed the ridge trail from Megiddo instead of preceding to the Great Trunk Road along the coast," Leo cautioned.

"Wouldn't that mean that they're ahead of us on the road to Sebastian?" Tom asked.

"Possibly, but the ridge trail is harder going with fewer water stops and a greater chance of being ambushed by brigands and pursuing auxiliaries," Leo replied.

"What if Damien intended to travel beyond Sebastian to Jerusalem?" Jeez inquired.

"I'm not sure why that would be the case, but if that were true, the Central Ridge Road starts in Sebastian and runs straight to Jerusalem," Leo observed.

"Damien might also set up an ambush of his own at the top of this ridge," Tom speculated.

"Keep your eyes open. Anything is possible," Leo cautioned.

Nervously, Leo led them up to Mount Gilboa,

where she dismounted to let her horse rest next to a spring. Tom and Jeez soon caught up and likewise dismounted.

Looking east back over the valley, Tom saw Jezreel, but hoped without evidence to see Tribune Claudius and his men.

"We're at least a half-day's ride ahead of any relief team traveling from Sepphoris," Tom observed.

"We're on our own," Jeez responded.

"What is that mountain north of us?" Tom asked.

"Actually, Mount Carmel is more northeast of us. That is where the Prophet Elijah confronted the four hundred and fifty prophets of Baal and the four hundred prophets of Asherah, and proposed a cook-off to see whose god would answer prayers to burn up the sacrificed bulls," Jeez recounted.

"Right. God answered Elijah's prayer while the prophets of Baal and Asherah cut themselves and prayed in vain. Queen Jezebel wasn't pleased when her prophets lost and were slaughtered by the people at Elijah's instruction," Tom noted.

"Not pleased is an understatement. Jezebel vowed to execute Elijah by the end of the day, and he ran for his life," Leo explained.

"Scary lady!" Tom remarked.

"Herodias and Jezebel share a common temperament," Leo observed.

"Super. And we are supposed to convince Herodias to arrest Damien?" Tom asked.

"That's the plan." Leo replied.

After taking a few gulps of water from the spring and watering her horse, Leo urged Tom and Jeez to do the same. Once they were done, she mounted her horse and returned to the trail to head west towards Sebastian.

Chapter Ten

Towards evening, Leo led Tom and Jeez up the foothills on the trail that led to Sebastian.

"Why is Herodias so influential in Sebastian and not her husband Phillip, whom they call Herod II?" Tom asked.

"Phillip and Herodias lived in Rome in the final days of Herod the Great and avoided the battles to succeed him when he died. When Herodias became homesick and returned to Sebastian, Phillip stayed behind in Rome, probably fearing the jealous and treacherous relatives who had seized power after Herod's death," Jeez volunteered.

"So, Herodias had more stones than her husband and became homesick?" Tom asked.

"Essentially." Jeez replied.

"The rumor was that before he departed for Rome, Phillip had called together his three most loyal stewards and divided his fortune among them to administer in his absence. Two of the three made him fantastically wealthy, but the third simply hoarded the money. When Herodias returned to Sebastian, she collected the proceeds from Phillip's stewards and kept her husband on a parsimonious allowance," Leo recounted.

"No more wild parties for Phillip. It sounds like Herodias is both ruthless and ambitious," Tom concluded.

"That's Herodias. She plays the temptress, manipulating men to get what she wants. No one in Israel dares defy her," Leo recapped.

∞

With nightfall, a bright moon illuminated the trail. Leo dismounted to walk her horse silently past local villages and to avoid any stumbling. Tom and Jeez followed suit.

"How far do we have to go?" Tom inquired.

"If you check out the ridge ahead, there is a flicker of light now and then, probably from torches held by the night watch on Sebastian's walls," Leo answered.

"So, we are almost there?" Tom inquired.

"We should be able to sleep outside the walls well before then," Leo responded.

Later, they arrived at the fortress walls surrounding Sebastian. They announced themselves to the night watch, tied up their horses, and leaned against the walls before falling sleep wrapped in their cloaks.

∞

At the break of dawn on Wednesday, Leo, Tom, and Jeez were awoken by Tribune Marcus and an auxiliary.

"I don't recognize you. Who are you?" Tribune Marcus inquired.

"We're deputy auxiliaries from the Sepphoris cohort. We have a warrant from Centurion Marcellus that authorizes the pursuit of four fugitives, who murdered the family of a centurion in Sepphoris," Jeez said, handing Marcus the warrant.

"I see," Marcus said, reading the warrant. "Follow me."

"Can someone attend to our horses?" Jeez inquired.

The tribune motioned to the auxiliary attending him, who led the horses to a nearby stable.

"This way." Marcus bolted through the open gate to the city and walked up to a large palace where the guard out front opened the door for him. Ivory carvings adorned the walls within, but especially decorated an outdoor throne set up under a canvas canopy in the middle of a large courtyard. An attendant escorted the group to stand in front of the throne. Another attendant disappeared briefly and returned with Princess Herodias, which prompted Marcus and Jeez to remove their helmets.

"Marcus, what brings you to the palace so early this morning?" Herodias inquired.

"These three auxiliaries from the Sepphoris cohort arrived during the night bearing a warrant for four fugitive auxiliaries accused of murdering the family of Centurion Augustine," Marcus reported.

"Why should I care about this warrant?" Herodias asked.

"Damien is one of the fugitives and they should

be here presently," Marcus responded.

"Damien, my illegitimate half-brother, is in trouble again? He promised to be a good boy if I let him join the Sepphoris cohort. What am I supposed to do with him?" Herodias said.

Marcus said nothing, but looked sheepishly at the ground.

"Well? Marcus, you're a tribune. What is the penalty for an auxiliary guilty of murder and desertion?" Herodias pressed Marcus, while staring at an attendant and motioning towards the gate.

"A tribune commanding such auxiliaries might impose the death penalty in such cases, even decimation. But theses auxiliaries belong to the Sepphoris cohort, so Tribune Claudius would be responsible for rending the judgment. Your responsibility is to hand them over to him if they come within your jurisdiction," Marcus responded.

Herodias stood up and shouted, "If Damien and his crew show up here, strip them of their weapons, chain them together, and send them to Claudius."

Herodias sat down and smiled coyly fanning herself, "Perhaps now, Herod Antipas will take notice and feel indebted to me."

"Very well." Marcus backed away and motioned for the three visitors to exit. He then followed them out of the palace. Once outside, he put his helmet back on and, without a word, led his visitors to the stable. There they mounted their horses and rode out of the gate.

∞

Leo led Tom and Jeez down the hill from Sebastian towards the Roman amphitheater and dismounted. She then led her horse over to a seat and sat down, motioning for them to join her. "Did you understand what just happened?"

"Herodias sent an attendant to warn Damien and his crew. Then she instructed Marcus simply to wait for him in Sebastian. Ordinarily, the local tribune would actively pursue such felons and bring them to justice. By ordering him to wait for them in Sebastian, she is protecting Damien," Tom observed.

"Marcus understood exactly what she was doing and ushered us out of town without even offering us breakfast or even oats for the horses," Leo observed.

"Knowing Herodias' reputation, Marcus may have acted to spare us her wrath," Jeez suggested.

"Perhaps, but why would Herod Antipas feel indebted to Herodias for what she did?" Tom asked.

"Herodias shares Damien's narcissistic tendencies, perhaps because their father, Aristobulus IV, was an alcoholic and abused his children. Damien's narcissism is displayed by becoming a cold-blooded killer while Herodias' shows up in her viciousness and promiscuity. Both of them are habitual liars," Leo reported.

"If Herodias won't help us and if Tribune Claudius hasn't caught up with us, what do we do now?" Tom asked.

"Let's get something to eat. Shechem is in the valley between Mount Ebel and Mount Gerizim, which is nearby. I hear that there is a good tavern between Jacob's well and Joseph's tomb," Jeez suggested.

"Clever. Where do you think Damien and his

crew would be if they were only hours ahead of us? I suspect that they would also be attracted to that tavern and that the staff could tell us all about them," Leo observed.

"If we pick up their trail, how will we communicate that information to Tribune Claudius?" Tom asked.

"We may not have to. Several Sebastian guards followed us down the hill, trying hard to stay out of sight. If Claudius arrives asking about us, they'll simply point towards Shechem," Leo noted.

"Good grief. We may not get out of this adventure without a fight, either with the fugitives or their guardian angels," Tom opined.

"Don't worry. In a pinch, we can retreat downhill east from Shechem to the Jordan River valley and return to Jezreel following the valley trail through Jericho," Leo explained.

"Actually, I was just hungry for some hot food," Jeez said with a smile.

Chapter Eleven

Leo mounted her horse. Tom and Jeez follow suit. She walked her horse down the trail toward Shechem.

As they rode along, Tom sought to jump start conversation with a question, "Why is Joseph's tomb in Shechem? I thought that Joseph was prime minister of Egypt."

"After Joseph's brothers sold him into slavery in Egypt, Jacob and his family camped near Shechem. One day his daughter, Dinah, ventured on her own into the city where Shechem, the son of Hamor the Hivite, raped her. Later, Shechem asked his father to arrange their marriage. In place of a bride price, Jacob asked that the men of the city be circumcised. When they were convalescing from the circumcision, Jacob's sons, Simeon and Levi, killed all the men and plundered the city," Jeez explained.

"Ouch," Tom exclaimed. "What a wickedly painful way to go."

"Shechem became the only land in Canaan that

Jacob ever owned, and it became the family's hometown. This is why Jacob dug a well there and Joseph was buried there," Jeez explained.

"Is Shechem known for anything else?" Tom asked.

"Actually, yes. Because of the sins of Simeon and Levi, among other things, Jacob bestowed family leadership on Judah—King David's tribe. Centuries later, King David's grandson, Rehoboam, wished to be crowned in Shechem after his father Solomon died, and Rehoboam gathered representatives of all the tribes for that occasion," Jeez explained.

"In other words, Shechem became symbolically important?" Leo observed.

"Presumably. The tribes agreed that they would accept Rehoboam as king provided that he lowered their taxes. When he refused, the ten northern tribes revolted under the leadership of Jeroboam. The breakaway nation is what we call Samaria. Jeroboam established his capital at Tirzah. The capital later moved to Sebastian. Thus, Shechem was the site of the division of the nation into Israel and Judah," Jeez elaborated.

"Thus, events at Shechem lead to the leadership of King David and the later division of the northern and southern kingdoms?" Tom posited.

"Yes. Shechem is both the symbolic birthplace and the place of dissolution of the United Kingdom of Israel under King David. If Israel is ever to be reunited, it should take place at Shechem, which is now called Sychar," Jeez opined.

"Cool story, bro," Leo said with a grin.

∞

Leo led Tom and Jeez down the windy slopes from Sebastian along wadis pushing ahead to the point that she had to stop and let them catch up.

"Leo, we need to stay closer to one another," Tom yelled.

"Let's pick up the pace, guys," Leo shouted back.

Leo disappeared around a bend in the trail and a moment later began screaming. Tom drew his sword, spurred his horse into a gallop, and raced around the bend. There he saw Leo surrounded by as many as a dozen brigands armed with clubs and knives. Tom let out a battle cry and rode right into them, swinging his sword over his head like a wildman. He wounded several brigands and startled the others. The wounded screamed in pain, and they all ran away, leaving him alone with Leo. Jeez followed shortly thereafter, wielding his sword.

"I thought that three lethal auxiliaries would be safe on the road," Tom smirked.

"One out of three ain't bad," Jeez joked.

"Let's get out of here," Leo suggested looking worried and spurred her horse to ride on.

∞

Approaching Shechem about a hour later, Leo stopped to survey the city and to rest in the shadow of Mount Ebel. Tom and Jeez rode up to her and stopped.

Leo leaned over to look at Tom. "You're a true friend and displayed real courage back there. The brigands cornered and scared me, but you scared the stuffings out of them. Thank you."

"You're the fearless one. Your leadership and trail-smarts make this trip possible. Most other women—most other men—would have just kept quiet and remained in Nazareth," Tom replied, turning his horse to look behind them. "One thing has bothered me after our little incident with the brigands."

"What's that?" Leo inquired.

"Those brigands were too easily spooked and not well organized. It was as if it were their first ambush. Do you think someone put them up to it?" Tom asked.

"You may be onto something. Shechem is a crossroad and a magnet for ruffians, but those brigands did not display the grit of hardened criminals," Jeez replied.

Is everyone all warm and fuzzy now? Let's get to it," Leo said, again spurring her horse.

∞

On entering Shechem, Leo asked locals for directions to the traveler's tavern. They simply pointed to an outdoor thatched-roof structure with clay seats next to wooden tables. Next to it on one side was a fire pit and grill. On the other side was a small stable with a similar construction.

When the three travelers approached the stable, an attendant offered to water and feed the horses for a small fee, which Jeez paid. They then walked over to the tavern and sat at one of the tables. A waiter quickly appeared, offering a large platter of flat bread, grilled mutton, goat-milk cheese, olives, lemon slices, and figs. The reasonable meal price included a jug of wine diluted with cold well water.

Jeez stopped the waiter. “Have you seen any auxiliaries here lately?”

“Four soldiers ate breakfast quickly this morning at dawn, then departed on the Central Ridge Road towards Bethel," the waiter responded.

“How would you describe those soldiers?” Tom quizzed.

“They were loud, rude men who claimed to belong to the Sepphoris cohort," the waiter responded.

“Why do you say rude?” Tom pressed further.

"They bragged about paying villagers to ambush travelers between here and Sebastian," the waiter responded. "They also left a big mess and threw wine on a servant girl who refused their advances."

Tom looked at Leo and said to the waiter, "Thank you. You have been most helpful."

Chapter Twelve

The three travelers relaxed and finished their breakfast. Afterwards, the waiter offers each of them a jug of water and a towel to freshen up.

Tom observed, "Is it my imagination or are the jugs here in Shechem different from those in Nazareth?"

"Good eye. Many of the people in Shechem were resettled from Assyria centuries ago and some, who wear pants rather than robes, immigrated from Parthia," Jeez explained.

"Is that why Jews and Samaritans don't get along?" Tom asked.

"Partially, but the bigger issue has a religious origin," Jeez explained. "In his farewell address, Moses directed Jews to offer blessings on Mount Gerizim and curses on Mount Ebel."

"It's odd that Moses would make that request because he never entered the Promised Land, if I recall correctly," Tom interjected.

"That's a head scratcher," Jeez affirmed. "It's said that Moses could see Gerizim from Mount Pisgah, where he died after looking into the Promised Land."

"Oh," Tom remarked.

"Centuries later, when Jeroboam became king of Israel and broke away from Rehoboam's Judea, he became concerned that if the people continued to worship in Jerusalem, they would also return to the king of Judea. Consequently, he built temples with golden calf idols on Mount Gerizim and Mount Ephraim, also known as Bethel. Those altars on high places became an anathema to the priests in Jerusalem, who referred to them collectively as the sin of Jeroboam," Jeez said.

"So, the prejudice against the Samaritans had both ethnic and religious roots," Tom continued, pulling on Jeez's thread.

"Yes. Still, some of the Northern prophets, but not all, worked to get the kings and people to return to worship of the living God. False prophets continued to speak on behalf of idol worship and foreign gods," Jeez explained.

"Religious activities in Samaria must be confusing," Tom observed.

"Confusing, undisciplined, and no help with daily living. It is easy to make a living as a prophet who tells people what they want to hear without sacrifice," Jeez continued.

"People need a living image of God to remain faithful," Tom observed.

"Worshipping golden-calf idols reinforces admiration of wealth and power, mirroring natural tendencies and local culture," Jeez said.

"If you're finished with breakfast, let's go," Leo urged.

∞

As they got up to leave, the waiter comes over to see them off. "I take it that you're traveling to Jerusalem to celebrate *Yom Kippur*?" the waiter said.

"Why do you ask?" Jeez replied.

"Pilgrims walking to Jerusalem from Shechem plan to leave this afternoon," the waiter replied.

"The road will be filled with pilgrims this afternoon?" Tom asked.

"Pilgrims, shepherds, and goat herders," the waiter responded.

"Why the shepherds and goat herders?" Tom inquired.

"*Yom Kippur* is the day of atonement, the holiest day in the Jewish calendar, when sin offerings are made that require suitable goats and sheep be available for sacrifice. The festival in Jerusalem lasts for the ten days after *Rosh ha-Shanah,* the Jewish New Year, that ends with *Yom Kippur,*" Jeez reported.

After Leo thanked the waiter, they picked up their horses from the stable and left for the Central Ridge Road.

∞

After passing out of sight of Shechem, Tom turned to Jeez. "I thought that the Samaritans had their own religion following the influence of Jeroboam?"

"Some people followed Jeroboam and his false prophets, but many remained faithful to the God of Israel," Jeez explained.

"Hence, the pilgrims of Shechem?" Tom continued.

"It was not just the sheep and goat herders. The pilgrims stand out because the married men wear kittels, white burial shrouds, to display their repentance," Jeez said.

"Will the pilgrims resent us for being Roman auxiliaries?" Tom asked.

"Not at all. The pilgrims will invite us to travel with them because the highway bandits will leave them alone," Jeez replied.

"Aren't the Romans resented as foreigners?" Tom said, pushing further.

"As foreigners, yes, but the Jews invited Rome into Israel to keep the peace because of the constant quarrels among the Herodians," Leo interjected.

"I never thought of Romans as peace keepers, except in the derogatory sense of *Pax Romana,* peace by the sword," Tom said.

"Roman strength is the envy of the world," Leo summarized.

"*Pax Romana* is fine, so long as Rome does not interfere with the Jewish religion, as the Greeks had," Jeez said.

"What did the Greek do?" Tom asked.

"Antiochus IV Epiphanes, the Greek king of Syria, tried to Hellenize the Jews about a hundred and sixty years ago. He erected an altar to Zeus in the middle of the temple and offered pagan sacrifices, including pigs, on the altar, a practice known in scripture as the abomination of desolation. It provoked the Maccabees to lead a revolt. Hanukkah, the Festival of Lights, and the menorah commemorate the success of the revolt," Jeez explained.

"Hmm. I always wondered about Hanukkah," Tom concluded.

"We'll hopefully stay ahead of the pilgrim traffic," Leo said. "Let's pick up the pace."

∞

Leo led Tom and Jeez to push their horses from a trot to a slow canter. Inexperienced riders that they were, this proved too fast for both the riders and the horses. Tom had trouble keeping his breakfast down and had to stop.

“I can't keep this up," Tom dismounted. He handed the reins to Jeez, walked away from the trail, and threw up his breakfast. Wobbling, he sat down on a large rock.

“I'm with you," Jeez said, tying the reins of the two horses to a small tree. He took out a gourde of water, drank from it, and handed it to Tom as he sat down. Tom took a drink.

Leo walked her horse over to the rock, dismounted, and sat on the rock with reins in hand.

“Let's take a ten-minute break," Leo said with a smile.

Looking out to the next hilltop, Leo saw a pair of hooded crows circling overhead on the next ridge, calling out in the distance. Looking more closely she noticed four riders on the trail.

“Hey, guys. Check out that next hill," Leo said, pointing to the riders. “Our brisk pace is paying off. Damien and his crew are just ahead of us on the next ridge. What will we do when we catch up to them?"

"Tom, you look like you have something to say," Jeez shared.

"Obviously, we need help arresting Damien and his crew. Thinking about it, I came up with a two-part strategy," Tom said.

"Two parts?" Leo repeated.

"In part one, Jeez, you'll sneak past them and travel to present the warrant to Prefect Coponius in Jerusalem. This will assure that Damien has a welcoming committee when he arrives in Jerusalem," Tom began.

"What is part two?" Leo inquired.

"In part two, Leo and I will trail Damien and his crew, waiting for Tribune Claudius. If an opportunity arises, we'll steal their horses to slow them down and make it easier to arrest them before they disappear into Jerusalem," Tom said.

"Actually, the horses were stolen from Leo's family. As the only surviving family member, the horses are effectively her inheritance so you wouldn't be stealing," Jeez suggested.

"I like this strategy. Whether part one or two works, Damien gets his comeuppance, and both parts are doable and within our competence to pursue," Leo stated.

"Works for me," Jeez responded.

Chapter Thirteen

Jeez stood, mounted his horse, and said, "My part is easy. Damien has never seen me dressed as an auxiliary. I will pretend to be a courier and just canter past Damien and his crew. Couriers are common on this road—no one will suspect a thing."

"You aren't worried that it will seem strange that they don't recognize someone from the Sepphoris cohort cantering by?" Tom asked, standing up and taking the reins of his horse.

"They're likely to overnight in Bethel," Leo cautioned. "You can wait until the sun goes down to pose as a courier."

Tom looked at Leo. "Good idea."

Jeez dismounts.

"Let's follow them out of sight until sunset. When the sun begins to set, I will carry on like a courier. After dark, it is dangerous to ride quickly on these roads," Jeez announced.

"And we'll see if we can retrieve a few runaway horses," Tom continued.

The three auxiliaries waited until Damien and his crew passed out of sight over the ridge line. They followed them at a discrete distance to Bethel, arriving at the village just before sunset.

∞

Seeing that Damien and his crew stopped at Bethel, Jeez cantered his horse down the road past Bethel towards Jerusalem. Once out of sight, he slowed to a trot. No one in Bethel seemed to notice or care.

Jeez arrived in Jerusalem around midnight and checked in with the night watchman. He slept leaning against the wall near the Fish Gate, outside of the *Mishneh* quarter of the city and the Fortress Antonia.

∞

Leo and Tom found a stream outside of Bethel where they watered their horses and waited for Damien and his crew to eat and fall asleep.

You have been through a lot of trauma and, yet, you seem alert and focused. How do you do it?" Tom asked.

"When this is over, I promise you, I am going

to have a real cry. For now, I need to focus on bringing Damien and his men to justice. It is the least that I can do for my family." Leo responded.

"I feel your pain. My father was also murdered, but the last that I heard his killer was still at large. You, me, and Jeez have a lot in common." Tom observed.

Leo walked her horse over and sat near Tom. "You're right. I never thought about it. All of us carry the same pain."

Tom took her hand and they just sat together watching the sun go down and enjoying the cool of the evening.

At midnight, they walked into Bethel to find Damien and his crew asleep outside a tavern. The horses were tied up in a nearby stable. Leo and Tom quietly untied the horses and walked them back to the stream.

Each with a string of fresh horses, Leo and Tom mounted up and rode hard all night until they reached Shechem around day break. There they returned to the tavern to rest their horses and enjoy breakfast.

∞

Because of the *Rosh ha-Shanah* festival on the day before *Yom Kippur*, Jeez was awaken early Thursday morning when the Fish Gate opened before dawn. With so many preparations for the feasts that day, Jeez easily found a stable for his horse and ate breakfast at a tavern in the *Mishneh* quarter. While he ate, he recognized a rabbi walking past who had taught him during his *bar mitzvah* just before Passover that year.

Jeez ran up behind his teacher. "Rabbi Levi, do you remember me from your *bar mitzvah* classes last spring?"

"Jesus of Nazareth? Of course, how could I forget my favorite student? What are you doing in an auxiliary's uniform?" Rabbi Levi asked.

"My father, Joseph, was murdered only a week ago in Sepphoris, and I was drafted by the tribune of Sepphoris cohort to bring the men involved to justice. I have a warrant for their arrest to present to Prefect Coponius," Jeez responded.

"No one can get an audience with the prefect

this week because of the holy days, festivals, and crowds," Rabbi Levi responded.

"Damien and his crew will be here later today. What should I do?" Jeez asked.

"You mean that you have a warrant to arrest, Damien, the illegitimate son of Aristobulus IV?" Rabbi Levi asked.

"Yes. Why do you ask?" Jeez responded.

"You need to forget about that warrant. His father is best friends with the prefect, and it will only get you into trouble. Damien has been accused of many crimes over the years, and his accusers have all quietly disappeared. He was probably posted to Sepphoris because his father wanted him out of sight, out of mind," Rabbi Levi reported.

"What am I to do?" Jeez asked.

"I have another idea. Walk with me," Rabbi Levi motioned towards the temple.

"What's your idea?" Jeez inquired.

"Ananus, the son of Seth, is high priest and well connected with the Romans and the Herodians. He is looking for a good Jewish auxiliary to serve as his body guard and liaison with the prefect," Rabbi Levi said, walking across the *Mishneh* quarter.

"What about Damien?" Jeez asked.

"Let me introduce you to the high priest. Once you make a few friends here in Jerusalem, you'll know better how to deal with Damien," Rabbi Levi talked with Jeez as they walked up stairs to a tunnel under the temple.

A pair of hooded crows circle overhead, calling out loudly.

∞

The tunnel led to a hidden chamber used by the high priest. Rabbi Levi led Jeez into the chamber, where they found the high priest, Ananus ben Seth, sitting at a table admiring himself in a mirror and practicing his remarks for the coming ceremony.

Looking up at Rabbi Levi, the high priest is annoyed. "Why have you brought an auxiliary into my chamber?"

"You asked me to propose a good Jewish auxiliary to serve as your body guard and liaison with the prefect," Rabbi Levi responded.

The high priest looked at Jeez, then waved Levi and everyone else to leave the room. When everyone had left the room, his face became contorted in obvious anger.

"I know who you are," the high priest said.

"That's what Damien said after he murdered my father, Joseph," Jeez replied.

"You already knew what would happen. It's your fault," the high priest responded.

"Knowledge is not causal. You're judged on your response like other men, not relieved of responsibility because I already knew. You retain free will under law," Jeez responded.

"Free will under law?" the high priest grinned.

"Damien's past is catching up with him. He will be turned over to the authorities for his crimes," Jeez said.

"What does that have to do with me?" the high priest asked.

"The law defines your role until the veil is torn," Jeez responded. "After that, God will abandon the temple, Jerusalem will be destroyed, and the people of Israel will be scattered."

"Why would God allow that? Jerusalem is his silk cloak; the temple is the sapphire necklace around his neck," the high priest said.

"Hoarders of God's truth, like those who turn their backs on God, are worse than those that sacrifice their children, practice abominations, or murder brothers and sisters. They must— like Cain—suffer the curse of diaspora," Jeez said.

"You dare to cite the Books of Moses to me?" Angry, the high priest waved him off. "Go preach in Galilee."

Jeez left the high priest's chamber by way of the tunnel and returned to the *Mishneh* quarter. He walked to the stable, attended to his horse, and left by way of the Fish Gate for the Central Ridge Road to Bethel. He rode out of the city, found a shaded spot along the road near a spring, and changed into his robe.

ACT FOUR

Chapter 14

Jeez sat on a stone by the spring watching a Balken Pond turtle sun itself on a fallen tree eying numerous dragonflies and damselflies that circle above with its mouth open. His horse grazes nearby until mid-afternoon when Damien and his crew come walking along the Central Ridge Road. A pair of hooded crows circle overhead, calling out.

When they draw near the spring, Tom and Leo ride up quietly with Tribune Claudius and his men close behind them. They watch an irritated Damien as he approaches Jeez along the road.

"Jesus of Nazareth, what do you have to do with me?" Damien said.

Jeez said nothing but wrote with a stick in the sand in front of him.

Damien came closer and drew his *gladius,* repeating his question. "Jesus of Nazareth, what do you have to do with me?"

"Why did you and your crew murder the Centurion Augustine and his household, and kidnap his daughter?" Jeez asked.

"The centurion scourged me and my crew, though he was beneath my station. He deserved his punishment," Damien responded.

"Did the centurion act on his own authority?" Jeez inquired.

Damien became enraged and shouted, "I am the son of Aristobulus IV. The centurion was beneath my station."

"Consequently, Centurion Augustine hurt your pride by carrying out his duty, lawfully prescribed by Governor Antipas, so in cold blood you murdered Augustine and his entire household, and sold his daughter as a Parthian slave?" Jeez asked.

Damien's eyes bulged, he screamed, and with sword in hand he ran towards Jeez. Tribune Claudius launched forward, drew his sword, and cut Damien down. In a single motion, Claudius' men attacked and beheaded Damien's crew as they stood fixated on Damien.

Leo covered her eyes and wept. Tom sat on his

horse stunned. Jeez looked up from his stick unmoved.

Tribune Claudius' men stripped the Damien and his crew of their uniforms, *gladii*, and helmets, and left their bodies in the sun as food for jackals.

Tribune Claudius cleaned his hands in the spring as Jeez approached. The turtle silently slides off the tree into the water.

"As the sole heir of Centurion Augustine's household, Leo should inherit the horses that Damien and his crew stole. This is what Tirzah argued before Moses in the Book of Numbers." Jeez observed.

"I know nothing of Tirzah or Moses," Tribune Claudius said. "It is simple justice that Leo should inherit her father's horses."

"I have another request." Jeez said. "Since we are already here, may Tom, Leo, and I have permission to celebrate *Yom Kippur* in Jerusalem?"

"Go with your friends and celebrate *Yom Kippur*. Report to me in Sepphoris when you return." Claudius left for Sepphoris with his men.

Leo, Tom, and Jeez returned to the *Mishneh*

quarter to find a stable for their horses and a tavern to enjoy the *Yom Kippur* eve meal. They spent the night near the Fish Gate under the eye of the night watch.

∞

Friday morning, they rose early and participated in the day's fast. Jeez led them out of the *Mishneh* quarter, following the steps shown him previously by Rabbi Levi. Because of the required ritual bathing, Leo could not enter the temple. As a gentile, Tom was likewise precluded from the temple.

"Where are you taking us?" Tom asked.

"Neither you nor Leo can enter the temple, but we can watch the *Yom Kippur* service from the temple portico." Jeez responded.

"I thought that the service was in the temple." Leo asked.

"It is, but the priests, led by High Priest Ananus ben Seth, can be seen processing in." Jeez reported.

"Then what?" Leo said.

"Periodically, Rabbi Levi comes out to read an account about what is going on inside." Jeez said.

“Like what?” Tom asked.

“Rabbi Levi explains the meaning the sacrifices, changes and types of garments, the ritual washings, and the prayers going on inside.” Jeez reported.

“What is the big deal?” Tom asked.

“The purpose of the *Yom Kippur* ceremony is offering sacrifices on behalf of the nation for the forgiveness of sin.” Jeez responded.

"How will we know if God accepts the sacrifices?" Tom asked.

“If the sacrifices are accepted, the high priest will emerge safely from the Holy of Holies. If not, he will need to be dragged out by the cord attached to his ankle.” Leo remarked.

“The temple priests maintain a monopoly on forgiveness of sin, much like the merchants in the gentile court maintain a monopoly on the sale of acceptable sacrifices," Jeez observed.

“Can’t I just pray to God and ask to be forgiven?” Tom asked.

“Yes, but if you say it out loud here today, you'll

be arrested by the temple guards and charged with spreading heresy, a charge taken very seriously," Jeez advised.

Shocked, Tom stared at Jeez as if the wheels in his head were turning. After a few seconds, he blinked and said, "Who are those people over to our right?"

"The man sitting on that fancy chair under the umbrella is Prefect Coponius. The people standing near him are members of the Herodian family hoping to be noticed," Leo remarked.

Rabbi Levi noticed the three auxiliaries standing on the portico. During his next trip into the temple, he reported Jeez's presence to the high priest.

∞

Before the final drama in the ceremony, Jeez motioned to Tom and Leo to leave early to avoid the post-holiday traffic. They walked down in the steps to the *Mishneh* quarter, retrieved their horses, and headed out the Fish Gate. At the gate, the guard stopped them.

"Be careful on the road," the guard cautioned. "Four members of your Sepphoris cohort were killed yesterday within walking distance of the city walls."

Jeez handed the guard the warrant for Damien's arrest. "Those four men resisted lawful arrest and were executed yesterday afternoon near the spring."

The guard looked up at Jeez white-faced but said nothing and handed him back the warrant. Jeez, Tom, and Leo exited the gate, mounted their horses, and rode off.

Later that day, the high priest called temple guards into his chamber with a stern look on his face. "I want you to ambush three young auxiliaries traveling on the Central Ridge Road."

"Outnumbered, those thee auxiliaries bested Damien and his crew. They are lethal killers," the temple guards responded.

"I will pay handsomely," the high priest responded.

"Perhaps, the Precept's men can handle this job," the temple guards replied.

The high priest waved them off.

Chapter Fifteen

As Jeez led Tom and Leo out of Jerusalem through the city gates, Tom turned to Leo and asked, "What happened to your four horses?"

"I sold them to Tribune Claudius, who paid in gold. He sent them back to Sepphoris with a couple of his men. Why do you ask?" Leo inquired.

"I wondered whether we should take the Central Ridge Road or an alternative road back to Nazareth. I doubt that Herodias will welcome us warmly if she learns what happened to Damien," Tom said.

"What? I was dreaming of dinner at the Shechem tavern," Jeez said, rubbing his stomach.

"One ambush near Shechem is enough for me," Leo chimed in. "Most pilgrims prefer the road through Jericho up the Jordan Valley."

"Why? What's the attraction?" Tom asked.

"People will tell you that it is to avoid Samaria, but it is also easier going. The valley has no mountains to climb, water is usually available, and the valley has fewer bandits," Leo reported.

"No mountains. No Herodians. No bandits. You've sold me," Jeez summarized.

∞

Concerned about Herodian reprisal for Damien's death, Leo was careful not to let their route to Galilee be visible from Jerusalem city walls as she led Tom and Jeez out of the city along the Central Ridge Road. After passing Gibeah, the hometown of Israel's first king, Saul, Leo led them on the road downhill to Jericho.

Several hours passed as they traveled. Bored with the rocks and scrub scenery, Tom asked, "Jeez, you love to tell stories, so tell us a story about Jericho."

"You'll like Jericho. It is a warm desert oasis. It is known for its springs, date palms, and fig trees. If Shechem is remembered for Israel's division, Jericho is famous for Israel's founding," Jeez said.

"Founding? Why?" Tom asked.

"God gave the Land of Canaan over to the Israelite people as a promised homeland. The timing of this gift was delayed until the sin of the Amorites was complete," Jeez explained.

Puzzled, Tom asked, "What was the sin of the Amorites?"

"The Amorites worshipped idols, especially Belu Sadi and Belit Seri, placing their priorities on things other than the living God, such as money, sex, and power. Scripture calls these detestable things an abomination to the Lord. Weak priorities lead to weak life skills and self-destruction," Jeez went on.

"Okay, how did Jericho stack up on all these things?" Tom asked.

"Jericho was the first Canaanite city—and probably the most formidable—that the Israelite people encountered after crossing the Jordan River into Canaan," Jeez responded.

"Formidable, how?" Tom pressed on.

"Jericho was the first mud-brick and stone walled city, and it was inhabited by giants," Jeez said. "When Moses first sent spies into Canaan to look at it, ten out of twelve of the spies came back too frightened to proceed into the land. Because of their lack of faith, God banished the people of Israel to the desert for forty years. Only the two spies who gave a positive report, Joshua and Caleb, lived to see the conquest."

"Why does the name Joshua sound familiar?" Tom asked.

"Joshua became Moses' commander-in-chief and led the nation of Israel into Canaan after Moses passed away. Jericho was the first city conquered. How it happened was an amazing story of faith that kids still sing about to this day," Jeez exclaimed.

"I remember that song. *And the walls came tumbling down,*" Tom sang, clearly off key.

"I take it that singing is not your strong suit," Leo joked.

"Ha, ha," Tom replied.

Leo pointed to Jericho in the distance. "Keep your eyes open. Jericho is a crossroads, like Shechem, that is a natural place for an ambush."

"Hey, just because you're paranoid doesn't mean they're not out to get you!" Tom said, amused.

"And, like Shechem, Jericho features some excellent taverns, as Joshua's spies learned," Jeez added.

"The city gates appear closed for the evening, but it may work to our advantage. Any reception committee may figure that they have the night off," Leo opined.

"Are you suggesting that Herodian retainers are lazy?" Tom said with a smile.

"Who me?" Leo replied.

"Let's take a break here until after sun down. No sense in making it easy for the Herodians to spot us as we slide by," Tom suggested.

"Wise counsel," Leo responded.

"Any food left in those backpacks?" Jeez asked.

∞

"Let's wait for sunset to fade into night and until clouds obscure the moon," Tom opined.

Leo and Jeez exchanged glances, then the three of them walked the horses down to the Jordan River and worked their way north around the city. When the moonlight returned, the trail became obvious from the skeletal remains of various animals and an occasional human skull scattered about. Some bones were still bloody and covered with maggots accompanied by an occasional scarab beetle.

In a moment of blind terror, Tom looked at Leo and Jeez, then he mounted his horse and drew his sword, "Lions."

Once out of sight of Jericho, Leo led them back to the road that ran along the eastern ridge while remaining on the alluvial plain. After riding for a couple of hours, they reached the turnoff to Shechem, encountering no one and nothing along the way.

After passing the turnoff, they rode up a small hill where they could see four wild, big-horned, Jacob sheep descending the rounding hills to approach the Jordan River through a field of tall grass. Out of the grass raced three lionesses. They seized two sheep that let out screams. The lions dragged the two dead sheep into an open field and gathered to feed.

"Let's get out of here while the lions are busy," Leo said.

Leo led Tom and Jeez nervously past the lion feast. Just as it seemed that the danger had passed, they heard a whoop and laughing sounds across the Jordan River.

The lions stood up. More than a dozen spotted hyenas appeared near them in the clearing. Lions roared and lunged at the hyenas, then retreated. The hyenas growled, baring their teeth. The lions made one last display of impotence, roaring and clawing the air, then ran off into the tall grass. Within seconds, the hyenas began gorging themselves on the dead sheep.

Leo led Tom and Jeez to gallop north on the road. Once the field of death was out of sight, they slowed their horses to a walking pace.

"Phew," Tom said.

When they reached the turnoff to the city of Tirzah, Leo turned and said, "I have had enough of lion country. Let's get back to the ridge road."

Tom and Jeez said nothing but followed her lead. At daybreak on Saturday, they reached Tirzah and found a tavern where they could stable the horses and have breakfast.

∞

The three veterans find a table, remove their helmets, and sit, exhausted from a long night without sleep.

Tom asked Jeez, "How can the temple priests maintain a monopoly on the forgiveness of sins?"

"The law places concrete boundaries on sin and the temple rituals offer concrete measures to atone for sin in the context of covenantal relationship, but they are not enough," Jeez explained.

"Why not enough?" Tom asked.

"God wanted a relationship with his people. The temple priests converted the relationship with God into a business transaction on which they held a monopoly. These transactional relationships cut out the role the human heart. Like a good father, God wants a loving relationship with his sons and daughters," Jeez explained, "not an arm's length transaction."

"It sounds like the rituals outlived their usefulness," Tom observed.

"Not entirely. Even the patriarchs managed to

develop a relationship with God, much like some people have used the Mosaic covenantal rituals to develop their relationship with God. But as the Prophet Jeremiah said, "God wants his law written on human hearts. A new covenant was required to expand the relational vocabulary and to render this new language meaningful to more people," Jeez explained.

"What you're saying is that people need to be convinced of their sin before they can understand their need for forgiveness. Sin, transgressions, and iniquity are not just meaningless, churchy words; they impede our relationship with God and other people. If people can't describe sin, they won't see a need for forgiveness," Tom observed.

"Exactly. One can't be forgiven if one does not know about and admit their sin," Jeez said.

∞

"How can I forgive Damien who murdered my family and sold me to Parthian slavers?" Leo asked with obvious bitterness in her voice.

"Damien has paid the penalty for his sin, which

is death. You played a key role in bringing him to justice. Your obligation to avenge their death is complete. What do you believe is the role of forgiveness? Jeez asked.

"Are you a rabbi, answering a question with a question?" Tom interjected.

"Tom, let me answer the question," Leo asked. "Forgiveness? My heart is still bitter. I have seen friends consumed by such bitterness. Can it be that forgiveness is the cure for my bitterness?"

"Damien does not deserve your forgiveness, but you do. In forgiving him, you purge the bitterness from your heart and leave no room for Satan to take root in your life," Jeez summarized. "Pray to God that you'll be able to grant Damien this forgiveness and ask God to fill your heart with his Holy Spirit."

"So, bitterness works like sin to frustrate our relationship with God?" Leo asked.

"Exactly." Jeez responded.

∞

"What about you?" Tom said, turning to Jeez.

"Damien murdered your father for no reason. Have you forgiven him?"

"I understand the need for forgiveness and have prayed to the Father that he would grant me the ability to forgive Damien. But it has been harder than I imaged," Jeez said.

"What does that mean?" Tom asked.

"My mind says *yes,* but my heart says *no*. I'm conflicted like anyone else. You and Leo have helped me grow into my forgiveness," Jeez said.

"Would it help you to forgive if you could return to the temple and offer sacrifices?" Tom asked.

"Yes, it would, once forgiveness has truly taken place," Jeez responded.

"What do you mean?" Tom pressed.

"A ritual is an outward sign of an inward meaning. The greater the cost of the ritual sacrifice, the more heartfelt the meaning. Heart and mind work together. However, the ritual loses meaning when it is generic, habitual, and without cost," Jeez reflected.

"Let's hit the road," Leo said.

After breakfast, Leo led Tom and Jeez northwest overland from Tirzah to the road from Sebastian to Jezreel. Once on the road, they were able to reach Jezreel before the city gates closed, and they spent the night there. By noon on Sunday the following day, they were back in Nazareth.

Chapter Sixteen

As Leo led Tom and Jeez into Nazareth, a crowd gathered to welcome the three young auxiliaries. Mary came running in spite of her obvious pregnancy.

Jeez dismounted and embraced his mother. As he did so, he whispered in her ear, "Joseph has been avenged. His murderer has been brought to justice."

Leo dismounted, handed the reins of her horse to Tom, and removed her helmet letting her hair hang freely. She turned to Jeez and said, "Leo is dead. I'm your sister, Mary Magdalene."

"You'll always be Leo to me," Tom said quietly.

Removing the pack from her horse, Mary Magdalene ducked into Mary's house to change. Moments later she emerged dressed as a woman and handed her helmet, *gladius,* and uniform to Jeez. "Please return this sword, uniform, and horse to Marcellus with my thanks."

Mary Magdalene assisted Mary in preparing some lunch for Tom and Jeez while a neighbor watered and fed their horses. After eating, Tom and Jeez said their goodbyes, mounted their horses, and set off for Sepphoris to report to Marcellus and return the things that Mary Magdalene's borrowed.

∞

Climbing the hill to Sepphoris, Tom and Jeez came to the spot where they had first met.

"It's time for you to return home," Jeez said, dismounting his horse.

"I know, but how?" Tom asked, likewise dismounting.

"When you're ready, just close your eyes and count back down from ten," Jeez said.

Changing subjects, Tom asked, "Why did you bring me here?"

"You asked for a tangible God. Has our time together been tangible enough?" Jeez responded.

"Too tangible. What will I do when I return home?" Tom inquired.

"Ask for God to grant you the Holy Spirit's guidance," Jeez said.

"Absolutely. It all sounds more real now . . . I will never forget you," Tom embraced Jeez.

"Nor, I you," Jeez whispered.

Tom closed his eyes. "Ten, nine, eight, seven ..."

∞

Tom woke still leaning against his mother's arm as the pastor's eulogy continued. He opened his eyes. He felt uncomfortable sitting, only to realize that he was, while dressed in his Sunday best, still also wore his *gladius*. He thought, *how am I going to explain this?*

The pastor finished his long-winded sermon, paused, and asked, "Would anyone like to share a remembrance?"

Tom stirred, looked around, and stood. He worked his way to the pulpit in front of the congregation, a hand grasping his *gladius* in its sheath.

Tom's mother gasped, displaying her who-is-this-guy look when she saw the *gladius,* which wasn't there when they left the house.

Arriving at the pulpit, Tom unsheathed his sword and held it over his head, pointing to the ceiling. "My father was a man who displayed obvious strength, but we never saw him yield his sword. He was quiet and polite, always putting our needs before his own. He was the man that I hope to become. Today, this very minute, I have resolved to become a police officer like my father." Returning his *gladius* to its sheath, Tom walked to his seat with all eyes on him and sits.

When the service ended, pallbearers carried his father's coffin out of the sanctuary. He and his mother processed out behind them. Looking into the faces of those attending, he spied Maddie. As they passed by her, Tom looked into her eyes and took her hand, "See you at the pole on Wednesday."

www.ingramcontent.com/pod-product-compliance
Lightning Source LLC
Chambersburg PA
CBHW061552250926
52052CB00010B/3171
* 9 7 8 1 9 4 2 1 9 9 5 1 9 *